"I can't wait to see how this looks when they flip the switch and light it all up tonight," Corrie said. "Want to bring your little sister and we'll all watch it together?"

"I'd like that," he said softly. *But…*

"Please say yes. It would be so sad to have to come down here tonight alone."

She had no father, issues with her mother, she was an outsider here. Corrie didn't just rattle Andy, she *needed* him.

Andy was a man who had made his life's work restoring things ravaged by time and neglect. He made things whole and right whenever he could. He couldn't change that about himself, but he had to be smart about it. Keep it under control. "Okay, stars this morning, lights tonight. But after that I have to get back on track."

"Okay, but just bear this in mind—if you stick to the tracks, you may miss some of the best scenery."

Books by Annie Jones

Love Inspired

April in Bloom
Somebody's Baby
Somebody's Santa
Somebody's Hero
Marrying Minister Right
Blessings of the Season
　　"The Holiday Husband"
Their First Noel

Steeple Hill Café

Sadie-in-Waiting
Mom Over Miami
The Sisterhood of the
　　Queen Mamas

ANNIE JONES

Winner of a Holt Medallion for Southern-themed fiction, and the *Houston Chronicle*'s Best Christian Fiction Author of 1999, Annie Jones grew up in a family that loved to laugh, eat and talk—often all at the same time. They instilled in her the gift of sharing through words and humor, and the confidence to go after her heart's desire (and to act fast if she wanted the last chicken leg). A former social worker, she feels called to be a "voice for the voiceless" and has carried that calling into her writing by creating characters often overlooked in our fast-paced culture—from seventysomethings who still have a zest for life to women over thirty with big mouths and hearts to match. Having moved thirteen times during her marriage, she is currently living in rural Kentucky with her husband and two children.

Their First Noel
Annie Jones

Steeple
Hill®

Published by Steeple Hill Books™

STEEPLE HILL BOOKS

**Steeple
Hill**®

Recycling programs
for this product may
not exist in your area.

ISBN-13: 978-0-373-87635-8

THEIR FIRST NOEL

www.SteepleHill.com

Printed in U.S.A.

In his heart a man plans his course,
but the Lord determines his steps.
—*Proverbs* 16:9

For Theo Anderson, writer, musician, son.

Invisible Ink
I keep filling up notebooks
With words I never sing
Creativity
Invisible ink

This is the song where realization hits me
I'm not the child I thought I would be
Listen close now,
I have a story to share with you

—Theo Anderson (6/14/91–11/11/09)

Memorials to:

Theodore Anderson Memorial Fund
for adolescent bipolar research
200 First Street
Rochester, MN 55905

Chapter One

"I'm out of time, nearly out of money, and if you look at what I'm trying to accomplish—completely out of my mind." Andy McFarland, his heart so heavy he could hardly breathe, stood in front of the two-story picture window in the old Snowy Eaves Inn and began a prayer that he had no idea how to finish. What did he want, really? What did he *need?*

If he had the answers to those questions then he'd do as he always did, collect the pieces, analyze the situation and do what had to be done. But at this point…

He looked around the nearly sixty-year-old inn where he was living as he restored it to its former charm and character. The lobby was rough but in good shape. So were the parts of the inn unseen from where he stood—the upstairs bedrooms and completely remodeled kitchen. But the dining room, currently little more than a large, lodge-like gathering room, stood in several stages of disarray. The old water-warped hardwood floors had been pried up leaving recently smoothed-over concrete in their place. The walls that had been harboring mold, poor insulation and potentially unsafe wiring—a fun little surprise they didn't find until deep into the renovation—had been demolished. Now only the wooden framework remained, leaving the room looking skeletal, almost desolate. It was…

Hopeless? A lost cause? Impossible? He turned again to the large windows that overlooked the secluded woods of his beloved and familiar Mt. Piney, Vermont. He shook his head, unable to find the right words.

A brilliant flash of lightning illuminated the abandoned tools left earlier in the day when the weather had gone foul and his workers left because they couldn't get anything done with electricity going in and out. A gust of wind rattled the windows. Andy felt the power of that gust through every inch of his six-foot-two-inch frame, but knew it was his predicament, not the weather, that had him shaken to the core.

The place that he had thought would be a showcase for his work and provide for his family for years to come had taken all his time, talent, a handful of construction loans and most of his savings. Two weeks after it was supposed to have opened for the season, the Snowy Eaves Inn and his life seemed stuck in an unfixable fix.

He shut his eyes and whispered the only kind of prayer he had left within him, "Please…help me."

Lightning tore across the winter sky. The flash illuminated the huge windows, casting his reflection back at him. Gone was the boyish twenty-seven-year-old with the cocky I-can-handle-whatever-life-throws-me attitude that he wore in his ready smile, the angle of his shoulders and his eagerness to take on tasks that others backed away from. Looking back at him was the image of a man who had planned so well, promised so much and now stood on the brink of failure.

The lights flickered and the expansive lobby went pitch dark.

"Great," he groaned and rubbed the heels of his calloused hands into his weary eyes. "I ask for help and get—"

"Andy? I don't like this, make it better!"

The power came back with a rumble and a hum. Andy turned to find his ten-year-old sister wearing pink pajamas and clutching her beloved sock monkey running down the sweeping stairway that emptied into the space designed to welcome guests into the inn. Her coal black braids flew behind her and her bare feet slapped over the polished concrete floor.

"You're supposed to be in bed," he told the child his mom had adopted from China as a toddler when Andy was nearly seventeen years old.

"Can't sleep. I'm scared." She threw her arms open wide and came sliding in to grab him around the waist and bury her face in his side. The dangling arms, legs and tail of the old stuffed toy that Andy had given her, one of his own childhood favorites, batted against his leg. "Buddy Mon-Kay is scared, too."

"Scared? Are you kidding me?" He cupped her delicate chin and cheek in his palm to protect her freshly washed face from his work-dirtied flannel shirt. "Greer McFarland, you're the bravest kid I know. You can't make me believe a little storm—"

"It's not the storm. It's this place." Her tiny, worried voice rose and echoed slightly against the vaulted ceiling.

"It's all echo-y down here and upstairs in my room, my night-light is going off and on by itself. Besides that, we're all alone out here in the woods. Something could get us!"

"First, we're never all alone," he reminded her. "God's always with us. And as an added bonus, you have me here to protect you."

"And pray with me?"

His chest ached at the thought of the desperate prayer he had just uttered. He was in this mess deep and that had him more scared than anything this sweet, sheltered child might dream up, even in a half-finished old landmark inn, deep in the Vermont woods. Still, he had just prayed for help to keep his commitments, what greater commitment could he have than to care for his family? He would not fail at that.

He exhaled slowly then knelt beside her. "And pray with you."

She grinned and held her hand out for him to take.

His large hand engulfed her small one.

She gave a sideways glance toward the limp sock monkey slumped over her arm.

Andy hesitated a moment. He shook his head then placed his other hand on the head of his old pal, Buddy Mon-Kay. That completed the prayer circle.

In her innocent way, Greer asked the heavenly Father to watch over them and to keep them safe. When she finished each sentence she gave Andy's hand a squeeze, and he repeated after her in his own fashion.

"And also bless Mommy and bring her home as soon as possible," Greer said.

"Bless Mom, bring her home safe." He avoided

mentioning just how soon, or how long it might be before his mother could return from her latest overseas trip helping fellow adopting parents. He loved his mom with all his heart and he really believed in her cause, but her timing left something to be desired. Just thinking of that made him huff out an agitated sigh.

"And make Andy less grouchy," Greer added.

"Make…" The kid got him. He'd been standing in prayer with her and thinking, not about her needs or about submitting to the Lord, but about his own petty inconveniences. He managed to dredge up a smile, even as he kept his eyes closed and head bent and repeated the request, "Help me be less grouchy."

"By giving him a girlfriend before Christmas!"

"By…hey!" That far he wouldn't go. He could hardly cope with his responsibilities as they stood right now, adding a romantic interest?

Greer giggled. "Amen."

"Amen." He gave her nose a tweak then stood. "Now back to bed. The storm is almost over."

As if to defy him, the whole sky exploded with a light as bright as day followed immediately by a booming roll of thunder.

Greer hugged Buddy close to her chest.

Andy reached out to take her by the shoulder but before he made contact, the lights went out again.

She whimpered.

Another slash of lightning and then another sent long, eerie shadows dancing over the front desk and the furniture draped in canvas drop cloths. Thunder shook the windows. The front doors rattled as if someone was trying to break them down.

Only maybe that wasn't from the thunder, Andy realized, when he looked that way and the door swung open.

A dark figure loomed in the frame.

Greer screamed.

The lights came on again.

"Story of my life, I tell you. I came all the way to Vermont in December to see a real, honest-to-goodness snow for the first time in my life and I get a thunder storm." A small woman in clunky fur-trimmed boots and a well-padded hot pink coat staggered over the threshold into the lobby proper. "And there go my glasses fogging up."

She whisked off a pair of trendy cherry red glasses and gave them a shake, flinging droplets of cold rain as far as Andy's cheek.

He wiped his face with the back of his hand. "Excuse me, miss, but—"

She parted her wind-blown, chin-length chocolate brown hair down the middle like a curtain and looked up. Mascara smudged her cheeks. She squinted in his direction. She tried furiously, and pointlessly, to dry her glasses on her sopping wet, lime green polka-dot scarf.

Andy would have offered his shirttail or sleeve but he was covered with drywall dust and only would have made matters worse. At this point, not making matters worse seemed like a giant step forward, so he held his ground and asked, "Excuse me, miss, I know the article in the Vermont Travel Monthly said we expected the inn to be open the week after Thanksgiving, but we've had some…setbacks. I'm afraid we can't take guests yet."

"Oh. I thought…" She slid her glasses back on and peered at him. "Your website hasn't been updated. According to that, I should be able to get a quiet cozy room with the best view in Vermont."

"Web site?" Was she trying to lay the groundwork to argue her way into getting a room for the night? Coming from anyone else, he probably would have found that pushy. From this girl? He liked pushy. Pushy? Wrong word. Spunky. That was better. The difference, he decided instantly, was the unabashed optimism of her approach. "Yeah, well, I've been kind of busy and…wait a minute, doesn't my website say to check back for an official opening date?"

"Can't blame a girl for trying." She gave him the most sincerely sheepish grin he had ever seen.

"Are you a robber?" Greer shifted her weight behind Andy but when he looked down he saw she had stuck the sock monkey out as though he were asking the question.

The woman did not hesitate. She bent down and addressed the toy as if it were the most natural thing in her world to carry on conversations with monkeys made from socks. "No, I'm not a robber. I'm a baker. And you are…?"

"Buddy Mon-Kay," Greer answered for the toy.

"Nice to meet you Buddy, can I call you Buddy?" She actually shook the monkey's hand.

Andy smiled. It shocked him a little, given the way the night had been going that anything could get that kind of response from him. Shocked him and sent up a signal flare. If he didn't act quickly, this baker in boots might just convince him to let her stay in the inn overnight. Not a good idea.

"Look, I hate to sound, uh, grumpy, but you can't stay the night here." He took a step toward the door. "There are two hotels in Hadleyville—"

"Are there? Do they have websites? I wonder if I have cell service out here." She fumbled around in her purse and pulled out a sleek new phone. "I could just look them up on the web and…if you're sure you're not open?"

"If she's not a robber, then maybe—" Greer whispered.

"We are not open," Andy reiterated.

The young woman chewed her lip, clutched her phone close then smiled in a way of someone used to adapting her plans on a moment's notice, of making the best of a bad situation. "Okay. So I'll find a place in Hadleyville. No harm. I just thought since the door was open, I would stop in and see…whatever."

"I'm staying here, getting work done, guarding against—"

"People like me?" She cocked her head and held her hands out as if presenting herself as exhibit A.

"I was going to say guarding against construction theft. I don't see how I could have planned for meeting someone like you." He laughed and shook his head, his mood suddenly lightened. No, Andy knew for sure he didn't know anyone like this. And her soft, southern accent reaffirmed that to him. "Just who are you and what brought you to the Snowy Eaves Inn?"

"I was gonna tell you that." Greer tugged at the hem of his flannel shirt and whispered, "I think she's the answer to your prayer."

Andy looked down at his sister, a little embarrassed by her remark and the subject of the prayer she was thinking of, and whispered, "That's not how prayer works. Her showing up now doesn't have anything to do with me or that prayer."

"Maybe it does this time. You don't know God's business," Greer shot back.

"My name is Corrina Bennington. But everyone calls me Corrie." The water-logged waif stepped forward, extending her right hand. "I came all the way from South Carolina to Vermont to find my father. But I came here to this inn tonight to find you, Mr. McFarland."

"Me?" Andy couldn't begin to imagine what this woman was talking about. Had he done something wrong? Was more trouble headed his way? Prayer was not a wish list, but he had submitted himself to the Lord and now this new wrinkle had appeared. He couldn't dismiss it out of hand. Even as his stomach tightened into a sickening knot, he found himself sort of smiling as he looked at the bright face of the young woman and asked, "Why me?"

"Because I have a unique problem that I believe only you can help me put right."

If she had used any other term, he might have told her he didn't have the time or energy. But putting things right was Andy's calling in life. To a man on the brink of total failure, a chance to do what he did best and for someone clearly in a lot of need, how could he turn her away? "If that's the case, well, I can't rent you a room, but I can offer you a place to dry off and warm up while you tell me what you have in mind."

Chapter Two

Corrie would have thought that things were going exactly as planned. Except that Corrie never *planned anything.* What good would it do? Life was not a recipe that followed prescribed steps to create a picture-perfect result every time. She had learned this from helping her mom in the bakery and watching her cope with what the world had dealt her.

Life was messy and sometimes painful. It was improvised, fly by the seat of your pants, make do and know things wouldn't always work out the way you hoped. You had to rely on your wits to get by because you never knew when life would throw you a curve. You never knew when someone, even someone you loved, someone you believed loved you, would let you down. That's how Corrie's mother had raised her. Be prepared for the worst and you won't be caught off guard by the bad stuff.

But what about the good stuff? Wasn't it also possible that if you were open and not too set in your ways that you could sometimes be caught off guard by things like opportunity, joy and love? Corrie had always wondered that when her mother tried to teach her yet another lesson about the harsh realities of life. Unlike her mom, Corrie wanted to believe life was also full of wonderful discoveries if you were brave enough to go after them. Though until this little adventure, in her whole twenty-three years, Corrie had never been quite this bold.

She followed the man she knew from his postings on the inn's website into the lobby and took a long, sweeping look at the surroundings, then at the man she had come specifically to see. Talk about caught off guard.

Her pulse raced. She hadn't expected this Andy McFarland guy to be so big. Or so cute. Or young. Or to have his adorable daughter with him. But then she hadn't planned much except to come to Vermont and pray she could find her answers here.

But most of all, she hadn't prepared herself for the overwhelming awe she would feel at just coming through the doors of… "The Snowy Eaves Inn. I'm really here."

"Yeah, but *why* are you here?" The man stopped in a huge, darkened room with exposed framework and wiring where walls should have been. He stood there like a wall himself, only in faded jeans and a dusty flannel shirt. Big as life. Bigger, actually, in contrast to the huge windows with rain pounding against them. The occasional lightning flash in the distance highlighted the breadth of his wide shoulders. "You said something about a problem?"

Be bold. There is no recipe. If she gave him the chance, he would find a reason to rush her away and Corrie wasn't ready to leave yet. So she gripped the oversized bag tucked under her arm and met his question with one of her own. "*You* said something about drying off and warming up?"

"I haven't said anything yet but if I did…" interjected the little girl in pink jammies and jet black pigtails clutching the sock monkey tugging at Corrie's thick coat, "I'd say, can you make hot chocolate?"

"Are you kidding?" Carrie whooshed out one long, relieved sigh. This was perfect. Cooking always cleared her head and now having met Andy McFarland and finding him just a bit intimidating, she needed a clear head more than ever. "I grew up in my mom's bakery making every kind of sweet concoction you can imagine. Just point me to a kitchen and—"

"This way." The child clamped both hands around Corrie's wrist and tried to drag her across the spacious lobby toward a closed door.

"Wait!" Andy made a lunge. He caught Corrie by the coat sleeve.

That was perfect because Corrie needed to get out of the cumbersome outerwear. She happily slid her arm free from the heavy, wet sleeve then gave a twirl to slip the rest of the way out.

She felt lighter already, just not because of the coat. She was in the place she had dreamt of seeing for most of her life, she had a pretty good idea what she wanted to do and she had just made an ally. "Thanks. Once you hang that up why don't you join me and your daughter in the kitchen and we'll discuss the details of the job I have for you?"

"She's not my daughter!" he called after her.

That news shouldn't have made one bit of difference

to Corrie, but it did. It made her heart and her footsteps instantly lighter.

"I'm his sister, silly," the child said with a giggle as if it were perfectly obvious that the big lumberjack-looking, auburn-haired man and the delicate Chinese girl were siblings. "My name is Greer."

Corrie's clunky fur-lined boots—the ones she had had to order special since the stores in her tiny town in the southern most part of South Carolina didn't usually sell snow boots—scuffed over the grit-sprinkled concrete floors of the lobby and hallway. When they stepped into a large, totally dark room, the floor beneath her soles changed.

Greer hit the light switch and the room flooded with brightness.

Corrie gasped. Unlike what she had seen of the rest of the place, the kitchen was not just finished, it was gorgeous. Though totally updated, careful attention had been paid to getting the ambiance right, the way it must have felt from the time it opened sixty years earlier until the place suffered a fire more than a decade ago. "This must be almost how it looked when *they* walked in here all those years ago."

Corrie settled her bag gently on the butcher-block countertop as she swept her gaze over every inch of the expansive, immaculate room.

Greer skidded across the shiny, red-tile floor toward the huge double-doored stainless steel refrigerator, asking as she went, "How it looked when *who* walked in?"

"My parents." Corrie paused. She so rarely had a reason to use that term. Corrie's father had abandoned them both before Corrie was actually born and she had been raised by her mom who had never married. The concept of parents was, well, just that, a concept to her. "They worked here twenty-four years ago. It's where they met."

A lump rose in her throat to think of two sweethearts filled with hope and possibilities and love. They had been young. She knew that much. Right out of high school and they had planned to marry, promised each other they would be together for the rest of their lives. But things did not always go according to plans.

If she let herself, she could become a stew pot of conflicting emotions. Years of heartache, of wanting to please her mom and longing to know her father could clash with romantic sentiment then throw in a dash of excitement over what she had come here hoping to accomplish. To combat that, Corrie did what she always did when she didn't know what else to do. She got busy in the kitchen. "When I read online about this place reopening… I didn't even tell my mom about it. I just felt like I had to come…and now…did you see the look on your brother's face?"

Corrie spotted what was clearly the pantry and in it found a tin of cocoa, a bag of sugar and a bottle of vanilla. "I'm beginning to wonder if it was such a good idea, my coming to Mt. Piney without making more definite arrangements. I don't know why I did it, really."

She spun around to find Greer staring at her.

The young girl had set the gallon of milk next to the gleaming new professional-style stove then tucked both of her hands behind her back.

Practically bouncing up and down in place, she whispered, "I know why you're here."

"You do?" Corrie set the ingredients down, not sure what to make of that claim.

"Well, I don't." The deep, masculine voice came from the doorway.

Corrie startled but recovered quickly. Her years of training as a baker served her well. Food didn't wait for you, you had to keep on task and moving smoothly. She didn't miss a beat in the prep process, lining up the ingredients in the order they would be used. "Right now, I'm here to make hot chocolate. To do that I need…"

She began opening and closing cabinet doors, looking for the perfect pan.

"This?" Suddenly, Andy McFarland stood over her, his arms raised as he retrieved the perfect sized blue-and-white enamel pan from an overhead cabinet.

Corrie looked from the pan to Andy's face. What a good face. Steady, thoughtful, no nonsense. Whereas, what she was about to ask him? Wobbly at best. Totally impulsive. Maybe even a little nutty.

He lowered the pan slowly, circling her in his arms as he did. Just when he got into a position that was almost an embrace, he pushed the pan toward her, stepped back and cleared his throat. "You said something about needing me to find your father?"

"Actually, no." Corrie slid the pan from his large hands then turned toward the stove and got to work. "I said I came to Vermont to *find* my father. However, that isn't the only reason I came. The other reason I came, and why I came out to the inn tonight, *that's* why I want to hire you."

She poured the milk into the pan, set it on the unlit burner then went to her bag on the counter. She couldn't help playing up the drama a bit, so she paused long enough to give both Greer and Andy her best enigmatic look, which must have worked because they each leaned in with their eyes on her. She sank her teeth into her lower lip, took a breath and pulled out a box and from that, the only family heirloom she actually owned. "I want you to help me recreate this."

"Wow!" Greer moved in to get a closer look at the old snow globe that Corrie held up. "Where'd you get that?"

"My father gave it to my mother when they worked here twenty-four years ago." The water had gone cloudy. An air bubble had formed at the top and exposed the galloping horse weather vane on the high ridge of the peaked roof of the small plastic replica of the charming Swiss chalet-style inn. She brushed her thumb over the raised words: Snowy Eaves Inn, Mt. Piney, Vermont. The movement jostled it just enough to cause the first few notes of a Christmas song to chime out from the tiny music box inside the stand. "It plays 'The First Noel.' He gave it to her as a promise that he'd come for her in South Carolina and they'd spend their first Christmas together."

"You want me to build another inn?" Andy held his hands out to his side to indicate the building where they now stood. "I'd like to help you, Ms. Bennington, but I can't even seem to get *this* one finished. Sorry, but you came all this way for nothing."

"Don't say that," Corrie whispered, fighting back the tears.

Even though she knew he didn't mean she wouldn't find her father, the very words tapped into her biggest fear. She had come so far, worked so hard. She just couldn't let it all fall apart now.

She set the globe down on the countertop and turned back to the hot chocolate fixings. She dumped in the cocoa and sugar then realized she needed something to stir it up with. She opened a drawer and on the first try found a wooden spoon. She gripped it tightly and finally turned back to him, refocused on her first task, getting the man's help. "But you don't have the whole picture. I've been working for almost a year to be accepted into the Hadleyville Holiday Gingerbread House Showcase with an entry titled Christmas at Snowy Eaves Inn. I've got the aesthetics down, but it's the steep eaves, the way the second floor hangs over the first. It has those balconies on three sides, which don't balance well. It may work with wood and stone but… I can't keep the roof from sliding off, or the top from being, well, top heavy and tumbling over. I think your expertise could—"

"Whoa, wait. You want to hire me to build a gingerbread house?" He held his hands up, his expression caught between a scowl and a smile. "Are you kidding me? I'm up to my eyeballs in real renovations and you want me to just up and—"

"Yeah!" Greer went on tiptoe then sprang upward, clapping. "Do it, Andy! That would be so—"

The girl flung her arms wide midjump. Her hand hit the handle of the enamel pan. She gasped. The pan flipped. Milk and clumps of cocoa went sailing in a high arch upward.

Corrie dove for the pan, not sure if the milk might

have gotten hot enough to scald the child. "Be careful, Greer."

"Don't worry, I'll save the snow globe!" Greer's small fingers stretched for the object but instead of grabbing it, bumped it and sent the treasured keepsake skidding to the edge of the counter.

Corrie gasped.

The globe seemed to teeter for a split second before it flipped over the edge, somersaulting downward.

Corrie's heart plummeted with it. She took a hurried step forward to try to save it. Her boot hit a puddle of milk and she lost her footing.

Andy lunged forward to catch her.

She'd have rather he'd tried to catch the snow globe. She pushed off Andy's attempt at a rescue and thrust both hands forward to make a sort of safety net to catch the keepsake.

The glass of the globe went slipping through her fingertips. It hit the hard tile floor, base first, did a sort of hop then came down hard with a sickening crash.

Greer squealed and leapt backward, her hands on her flushed cheeks. "I am so sorry. I didn't mean to do it, honest."

Just before Corrie's knees would have hit the unforgiving glass-cluttered tile, Andy bent down and caught her. She fell nose first against his muscular shoulder.

The dust on the flannel made her sneeze.

"Remember what I always say about there being accidents and there being consequences, Greer?" he asked firmly even as he steadied Corrie back on her feet. "The globe breaking was an accident. The milk spilling was a consequence of your actions."

Corrie covered her eyes with one hand. Consequence or accident, she just couldn't look.

Greer said something so softly that Corrie couldn't make it out but the forlorn sound of it made her heart ache. She had been raised by a mother who often made her feel as if everything she did was wrong, or at least not quite good enough. Corrie understood her mother's drive to create a sense of self-reliance in her only child and she loved her mom, but she didn't want Greer to feel the way her mother had unintentionally made Corrie feel.

She rubbed her eyes with her thumb and forefinger then turned toward the little girl. Rally, she told herself. You can't change what happened, only the way you respond to it. "Sweetie, you're barefoot and there's glass everywhere, maybe you should skedaddle."

"Yeah. Why don't you head back to bed?" Andy suggested, giving her a tender nudge. "I'll take care of this."

Greer sniffled and looked up at the big man bending down to lend her comfort. She managed a wavering smile and gave him a nod that seemed to say she believed he could take care of the mess and whatever consequences came with it.

Corrie wished that even once in her lifetime she had known that kind of trust in another human being. Her mother had always pushed her to be strong, be self-sufficient… "Be careful," she called out to the girl. "And don't feel bad. Things happen."

Greer picked her way across the floor and out of the room.

Corrie sighed. She still couldn't stand to look at the

broken bits and pieces of the only memento she had ever had of her father.

"Leave this with me. I'll do what I can." He put his hand lightly on her shoulder.

She shrugged it off, not to be rude but to let him know that she didn't need his sympathy. "Things happen that you don't see coming," she said softly again. "What you do after that, that's what matters."

"I know the owner of Maple Leaf Manor in Hadleyville. Let me call and make sure they have a room for you." He went to the phone hanging on the wall. "That's not too far a drive. I grew up there. My mom and Greer live there. That's where my office is. With the rain letting up you can make it over there in twenty minutes or so."

He pressed in some numbers as he spoke to her, then quickly made the arrangements. After he hung up he told her, "You'll have a room waiting."

"Okay. I actually was on my way to Hadleyville when I saw the sign pointing the way here and…well, the rest is history." She pushed her glasses up on the bridge of her nose and sighed, adding, "Just like my snow globe."

"I meant it when I said I'll take care of this. I'll put this right." His hand cupped her shoulder again, this time firmly enough to let her know he wasn't going to be dissuaded from offering comfort. "That's what I do, you can count on me."

Corrie looked back and up, deep into his searching brown eyes. She wanted to count on him. On *someone*. Her whole life she had wanted to feel like she had someone besides herself to fall back on. "Does that mean you'll help me assemble the gingerbread version of the Snowy Eaves Inn?"

He looked at the ceiling, groaned and then finally met her gaze. "Okay. I'll do what I can. Meet me in my office tomorrow morning at nine and I'll give you some pointers, if I can. But do me a favor?"

"Sure."

"Don't tell anyone I'm acting as a consultant for a cooking contest. I'm having enough trouble keeping my reputation intact with all the setbacks and complications of this renovation without throwing that into the mix."

Chapter Three

Andy dropped Greer off at school at 7:30 a.m. then turned his big black pickup truck toward his office just off Hadleyville's town square. The trip wouldn't take more than two minutes. So why had he told Corrie Bennington he'd meet her at his office at nine?

It wasn't like he needed a lot of prep time to discuss the best way to keep a gingerbread house from falling apart. Use better support. End of story, goodbye.

He really needed to be back at the worksite if he hoped to get the place done in time for the newly rescheduled grand opening party slated for the evening of Christmas Eve. And yet, when he had hurried her to the door last night, trying to get her on her way so he could get back to the mess in the kitchen and try to sort that out, he had blurted out his office address and told her he'd be there at nine. Why?

The simple answer? The woman had rattled him.

"Some simple answer," he muttered sarcastically as he pulled up to a stop sign around the corner from his destination.

He was twenty-seven years old, a business owner, the man of his family since his dad died eight years ago. He spent his days on construction sites, or negotiating with customers and suppliers. He had helped raise his little sister when his mother's work took her out of town for weeks at a time. He had once taken over for his mom teaching Vacation Bible School to five-year-olds! He did not get rattled.

Especially not by a girl with wild brown hair and trendy glasses, bursting into his business bundled up in a bright pink coat and boots better suited to an arctic expedition than a rainy Vermont evening. He smiled at that memory. Then he turned the corner and busted out laughing.

There she was. Corrie Bennington—trudging down the sidewalk in that unforgettable coat and those clunky boots.

He pulled up alongside of her and hit the button to roll down the passenger window and called out, "You know, the weather forecast says no chance of snow whatsoever for today."

"Oh, hey!" She broke into a warm, genuine smile but didn't slow her pace. Her breath made moist little clouds in the nippy morning air as she said, "What's with that? I talked to my mom this morning and it's colder in the Carolinas than it is in Vermont!"

"My office is right up ahead. If you want to—"

"Can't stop and chat now." She gave him a wave and kept moving. "On the trail of a hot popover. Don't want it to get cold."

Get cold? The trail or the popover? Neither one made any sense to him. He pulled forward and took

his preferred spot in front of McFarland Construction
and Restoration. He got out and caught up with her, his
long legs easily matching her hurried stride. "You're out
and about awfully early."

"Ha! You call *this* early?" She was walking so fast
that the heat rising from inside her coat steamed up her
glasses slightly. "Back home I'd have already put in
more than a couple hours of work by now."

The bright coat, the determination, the puff, puff of
her breath put Andy in mind of the little steam shovel
determined to dig a cellar for the new town hall right
out of a children's book. Never in his life had he ever
thought of a woman in that way and to his surprise,
it made Corrie Bennington all the more interesting to
him. He stuffed his hands into the pockets of the khaki-
colored down vest he wore over his red-and-black flannel shirt and cheerfully kept up with her. "You said
something about a popover?"

"Word around the free continental breakfast at the
motel this morning was that anyone who helps the First
Friday Christian Fellowship Club string up Christmas
lights this morning for the big Light Up Hadleyville
tonight is entitled to real homemade popovers made by
honest to goodness Vermont church ladies." She pointed
toward a crowd of people shuffling around town square
a half a block away. "Yum!"

"You're going to crash a service project for a popover?" He paused.

"What crash?" She didn't hesitate as he fell out of
step with her, just kept her eyes on the prize and went
full steam ahead, calling back to him. "It's the first

Friday of the month. I'm a Christian. I like fellowship.
And I have a great eye for decorating, me being—"

"I know, I know, a baker." He had to jog a couple
steps to catch up with her again. "You've mentioned
that before."

"Besides…" This time she did stop, even did a half
turn toward him.

He had to pull up short to keep from slamming into
her and probably knocking her to the ground.

"Besides…" she began again more softly as she
looked up at him, all innocence and expectations. "I
came here to find my father. I don't have to tell you that
any records from the inn, particularly from before I was
even born, are long gone. I think it's time I got out and
asked around a bit. Somebody might remember him.
Somebody might even know what happened to him.
Maybe he's even a local."

"Your mom didn't tell you if he was or not?"

"My mom doesn't talk about him. I forced the issue
once, when I was thirteen. She tried to find him. I overheard her trying and when it didn't work out, then I
overheard her crying…for days and days. I never talked
about finding him to her again." She looked away for
a moment then turned her face upward and gave him
a hopeful smile, nodded toward the group gathering in
the park and started to walk again. "I got a name from
that, though. James Wallace. Did some looking around
on the internet. Didn't find him, but I did find out about
the gingerbread house competition."

"So you're using the competition as a kind of cover to
come to the area and see if you can find out more about
your father?" For something so simple, she seemed to

have made it awfully complicated. Andy's lips twitched as he tried to rein in a grin. That, he decided, was Corrie's biggest obstacle and one of her most endearing charms—a confounding mix of complex simplicity and simple complexity.

He should run from that, of course. She didn't really have a big problem with her gingerbread house. He could call out his advice right now and be done with it. Done with her.

He watched her striding purposefully toward the park full of unsuspecting strangers, hung his head for a moment, then took off after her, asking, "Does your mother know that's what you're doing?"

"I can't tell you she doesn't suspect I might try to find out about him. The truth is, I have been struggling between finding my own way back in South Carolina. I tried finding a way to fit into her business, but it's really small, just getting by and she doesn't need me there. Two years ago, I entered a local gingerbread contest and got the bakery some good PR. So when I found one in a small town just a short drive from the Snow Eaves Inn..." Corrie stopped again, blinked and tears pooled above her lower lashes. "Mom encouraged me to go. But she didn't offer any help looking for my father and I didn't ask. I *couldn't* ask. That's just the way it is."

Andy gazed into her sweet, fresh-scrubbed face. The openness and longing to have answers, the weight of her strained relationship with her mother, her longing to find herself, her place in the world and where she came from, it all cut through him. "Okay. You got me. I'll help."

She sniffled and her expression brightened. "You're going to string Christmas lights, too?"

He'd been talking about helping her with the competition but he realized she hadn't even considered that he hadn't planned to do that all along. He shook his head. She was so vulnerable. So fragile and didn't even realize it.

There was a chance that what this girl was undertaking could leave her shattered. He thought of the pieces of the broken snow globe that he had gathered in a box but could not quite bring himself to throw away.

"Yeah, I'll help string lights and then we'll go to my office and I'll see what all I can do to help you stabilize your gingerbread house." He winced a little as he said it. "But that's it. I have so much on my plate and nobody to help me, so I can't afford to vary my course any more than that, got it?"

She pantomimed crossing her heart. Then she grabbed his arm and headed for the crowd hovering around two long tables piled high with strand after strand of tiny lights in front of an oversized gazebo where, once upon a time, the town had held summer concerts and where, years ago, the town had put up an ice skating rink every winter.

It didn't take long for Andy to realize he wasn't the only person pleasantly rattled by the unruly energy of this southern belle of a baker. Almost as soon as he introduced her to them, she had the town's grizzled old bench sitters, the fellows who would give you the shirt off their backs but grumbled about everything from the weather to the ways of the world, hanging on her every word. It would have been the perfect time to ask if any of them knew her father.

Instead, when the mayor, Ellie Walker, who had been

in charge of deciding how and where to hang the lights in the park for the last eight years, threw up her hands to proclaim she had run out of new ideas and asked for input, Corrie rushed to the rescue. The two women put their heads together for a few minutes while the whole group shifted and huddled in the cold. The next thing Andy knew, the mayor ushered the pink-coated visitor onto the bandstand gazebo as a makeshift stage to make an announcement.

"We wanted the centerpiece of the town's Christmas decor to look like a confection, so who better to trust with the job than a sweet young baker, Corrie Bennington?" Mrs. Walker, a sturdy, stalwart type that Andy had never seen without two pair of glasses, one always on her nose and the other always on a chain around her neck, threw out her arms as if offering the world, or at least their little piece of it, to Corrie. "Her coming here a whole week early for the contest is a very special sort of Christmas surprise, I'd say. Corrie give us some directions, or ask us anything, we're ready for it."

All eyes fixed on her.

"I just want to say that I've been in your town less than a day and I already love it. Honestly, I think I loved this part of the country long before I got in my car to come here two days ago. I loved the idea of it. I loved the history of it, what little I knew, and am honored to be here and happy to pitch in."

The group applauded.

Her smile beamed brighter than a crystal and silver Christmas tree star.

Andy couldn't take his eyes off her. His mind should be on his own work, on what needed to get done today but looking at Corrie, all he could think was how much he hoped things worked out for her.

"And I'd like to ask…" She seemed to scan the faces trained her way.

Andy shoved his hands into the pockets of his vest and concentrated on her, trying to let her know she had his support in asking the crowd about her father.

Her slender shoulders rose then fell as she exhaled, her warm breath visible in the cold air. She pressed her lips together. Cleared her throat. She started to say something, paused, tucked her hair behind her ear then pushed her glasses up on her nose. At last she smiled. "I'd like to ask if anyone knows this song?"

She broke out singing.

The crowd laughed. Some scratched their heads. Some chimed in. But when Corrie came down the steps and began giving orders, all of them began to work together to get the job done.

Andy shook his head as he watched the dark-haired young woman move from the tables of workers to the grand bandstand. Her hands flitted delicately as she described how to drape and wind the strands, making Andy smile. Despite being a poorly outfitted little steam shovel of a person, she had style and graciousness that he hadn't found in any other woman he'd met, he had to admit that.

And that worried him. He had so much work to do that he didn't see how he could accomplish it all. He had a budding reputation as a master renovator to uphold and an inn that he had promised to open two weeks from today. Nothing Corrie was asking of him would further that goal. He really needed to hurry her along, give her his advice and then...

"I really did get here at the right time. They had two strings of twinkle lights with green wire instead of white." She tucked the coils of lights into her purse presumably to keep the decorating group from mixing them in the decor again. Then she grabbed Andy by the hand and began trying to pull him toward the grand bandstand. "And speaking of right time—time to hang the big light-up star shapes. We need someone tall and strong who won't try to override the plan. I told them I had the perfect man in mind."

He resisted. At least he had intended to resist. But when she grasped his big old work-roughened hand in her soft, supple fingers and she smiled up at him, he was done in all over again.

"C'mon." She tipped her head toward the waiting workers, her eyes sparkling with joy in what she was doing.

It was a temporary thing, he told himself.

He dragged his feet and feigned a protest.

Just this morning, he laid out a clear boundary in his mind.

She walked backward, laughing at his feeble show of reluctance.

When she left his office later this morning with whatever solutions he could provide, that would be it. He reinforced his decision silently. No more Corrie. Bye-bye, baker. He'd do what he could to help her, of course, but then...

"I can't wait to see how this looks when they flip the switch and light it all up tonight." She stepped up into the bandstand and did a twirl, her arms extended. When she spun around to face him again, she laughed lightly. "What do you say? Want to bring Greer out and we'll all watch it together?"

"I'd like that," he said softly. *But…*

"Please say yes. It would be so sad to have to come down here tonight alone."

She had no father, issues with her mother, she was an outsider here. Corrie didn't just rattle Andy, she *needed* him.

Andy was a man who had made his life's work restoring things ravaged by time and neglect. He made things whole and right whenever he could. He couldn't change that about himself but he had to be smart about it. Keep it under control. "Okay, stars this morning, lights tonight. But after that I have to get back on track."

"Okay, but just bear this in mind, if you stick to the tracks, you may miss some of the best scenery." She handed him a star.

He looked down at her as he accepted it and said softly, "That's over-simplifying the way of the world a bit for me, but I can tell you that I am enjoying the view right now."

"Thanks," she whispered just before she turned on her heel and pointed to the rafters. "Start hanging the decorations there and I'll supply the music to work by."

Chapter Four

Corrie went marching over the threshold of Andy's office singing the song she had launched into at the park—a bellowing parody of "Jingle Bells"—at the top of her lungs.

The brisk winter wind snagged the door and blew it shut with a *wham*.

She gasped in surprise and halted her song, midlyric.

Andy eased his way around her to the other side of the large desk that dominated the small room. He chuckled under his breath as he slid off his down vest and hung it on a brass hook on the back wall. "I can't believe you got that group of stalwart New England stoics to join in singing that song!"

"It's a reliable old way of getting a team to work together, sing an upbeat song." Every little object in Andy's office vied for Corrie's attention.

"It was also a pretty sneaky way of making it impossible to ask people about your dad."

She whipped her head around. Heat flooded her cheeks. "I…it wasn't…how'd you know?"

"The minute you put your foot on that gazebo you had everyone on your side, Corrie. They would have done anything you asked, and you asked them to sing." He turned toward her and leaned forward with both hands braced against his desk. "You didn't ask about your dad."

She dropped her gaze downward, staring at the toes of her boots. "I dreamed about doing this for most of my life and now that I had the chance..."

"Dreaming about something is not the same as preparing for it," he said softly.

If that same sentence had come from her mother's lips, Corrie would have felt scolded, like the world's biggest disappointment. Her mom would have meant well, but Corrie would not have taken it that way. Mother and daughter relationships were so complicated. The only relationships more complicated, Corrie figured, were between men and women. She met Andy's eyes and felt comforted instead of confounded by his words.

"I've had a lot of experience with dreams not measuring up to reality in restoring the inn, and in watching my mom help people get ready to become parents to their adopted children."

"I don't know if it was spending time with them, or because we'd talked about how badly my first attempt at finding my dad had gone, but I looked at those people and suddenly realized that while one of them might have some answers for me, this wasn't just about me." She fidgeted with the fringe on her green-and-white scarf. "These good people had their own lives. My father has a life. Maybe he has a wife and other kids around the area. I needed more time. I needed to find a better way so once I had everyone's attention, I had to think fast."

"You do that a lot, don't you? Shift gears." He held his hand out to take her coat next. "You think fast."

"I guess so." She didn't know if he meant that as a compliment or a criticism, or both. Or maybe neither. She was usually pretty good at reading people, but she just couldn't get a handle on this guy. Probably because he'd gotten tangled up in her feelings about finding her father and his ties to the inn where her parents had met. That was it. That was all.

She wriggled to free herself from her heavy coat, but her arm got twisted. Her scarf snagged across her throat. She couldn't quite reach it with her arms pinned at awkward angles by her sleeves.

"Here, let me help." Andy stepped up and unwound the scarf, then with one gentle upward tug he set her coat right and slipped it from her shoulders. "You really don't have a lot of practice with winter clothing, do you?"

Corrie felt immediately cooler and infinitely uncooler at the same time. "If it counts for anything, I almost never get that snarled up in my flip-flops."

He laughed.

She liked his laugh. It didn't just put her at ease, it put things right. She stepped away from her coat and thanked him as he hung it on the hook next to his.

"Okay. We came here to talk gingerbread, so let's talk gingerbread." He swept out his arm to offer her the brown leather chair across from his desk.

She turned away, more interested in the books and

photos on his bookcase than in sitting down. "I think better when I'm moving, if that's okay."

"Okay." The wheels on the stiff-backed black chair on Andy's side of the unadorned metal desk creaked as Andy dropped into it. Paper crackled. His boots scuffed over the industrial-grade gray carpet. "I've gone over the drawings you gave me of what you want the finished building to look like."

"Uh-huh." In contrast with the unremarkable decor of his dingy office, the books and objects on his bookshelf presented an intriguing mosaic of business, cultures, faith and family history. She peered closer at a photo in a handmade frame of a red-haired woman hugging Greer. "Is this your mom?"

"Yeah." He barely looked up then went straight back analyzing her notes and sketches. He thumped the paper laid out on his desk. "I think the issue with the roof and keeping the second story stable can be solved with one pretty basic change."

"Really? Great!" She dragged her fingertips along the spines of his books. The topics ranged from architecture to vintage designs to a collection of works by C.S. Lewis. "Were you able to figure that out by comparing what I came up with to your actual blueprints of the inn?"

"I don't have blueprints of the inn." He folded his arms over his chest. "The old place has been worked on and passed from owner to owner over the last six decades. No blueprints exist anymore, as far as I know."

"Oh." She turned to face him. He looked so substantial standing there. "Then how are you doing all the renovations on the place to make it like it was before the fire?"

He cocked his head. "The fire didn't actually destroy the inn. The fire started in one of the little guest cottages and took out all six of them. The embers from that reached the back of the inn to the kitchen and office and they burned. The dining room suffered a lot of water damage but everything else was saved."

"That's how all the records were lost and why the kitchen is in such great shape."

"Yep. The cost of that and of cleaning up forced the original owner to sell and since then four different people have tried to get it up and running. They were able to fill enough rooms to get by, but they didn't get good word of mouth. I think that's because no one did anything but cheap cosmetic repairs, no one…" He squeezed his eyes shut and rubbed his forehead obviously trying to find the right word.

"Loved it the way you did," Corrie offered.

His eyes practically popped open. "I was going to say no one else had my vision for the place, but yeah, you pretty much summed it up. I have a special place in my heart for that old inn."

"So, let's do it justice with my contest entry." She slapped her hands together and rubbed them as she finally came to the desk, ready to get down to work. "What can we do to get my version of the place to hold together?"

"Easy. It's all about what we call the bones of the structure, and about your foundation." He stabbed his finger here and there on the page. "Looks to me like you're relying on fitting pieces of gingerbread together and gluing them in place with frosting when what you should do is use a wooden framework or maybe a Styrofoam model."

"That would be perfect!" She angled her shoulders back and rolled her eyes. "If I wanted to get disqualified before I even got the entry in the door."

"Disqualified?"

"According to the rules—"

"There are rules?"

"Of course there are rules." She scrunched up her nose. "It's a contest, silly."

"No, I mean there are rules and you didn't bother to share them with me? Where are they?"

"I don't know. On the website?"

"You didn't print them out?"

"Don't freak out, Andy. They're pretty much the same basic rules all these contests have. You have to keep a record of yourself making your gingerbread house by dated photos or video. No kits. No electrical lights or motors. Every part of the entry must be edible. I have the basics in my head, that's all I need."

"But…" His face actually went a little red at the thought of her not being a stickler for the rules.

She laughed and stretched across the desk to put her hand on his arm. She gave the strong muscle in soft flannel a squeeze. "It's okay. I'm not in it to win it. I just want to do my best and to honor the inn."

That last part got to him. She could tell by the way his pinched expression relaxed. No, not just relaxed, actually seemed to warm to the idea, or was it to her way of doing things?

"Hey, if you can restore the inn without blueprints or records of how it used to look, then you can help me figure out how to make a gingerbread replica of it without Styrofoam." She looked around her at the contrast of the businesslike office and the mementos of the not always all-business business man before her. "I know you can fix this, Andy. I believe in you."

She let her hand slip from his arm. Instantly, her fingers felt chilled.

His eyes met hers. Some of the former tension returned to his face. "All right. Sure. You have the rules in your head and I've got a new problem on my hands."

"It's not just in *your* hands, Andy." She stepped around the side of the desk, wanting to better illustrate her point that they were a team by literally putting them both on the same side of the desk that held the plans for the inn. "Remember, I'm with you in this."

"I know." He scowled slightly, rubbed the back of his neck then looked down at her. "Edible, huh?"

She used her shoulder to bump against his side. "If it helps, it doesn't have to taste good."

"I'll take that into account." He chuckled. "Oh, and by the way, I never said I didn't have records of what the inn looked like throughout its history. I said the blueprints are gone, and you were right when you said the records in the office were destroyed."

She froze mid second bump. "What do you mean?"

"That inn has been a part of this area for a very long time. People have had weddings there, reunions, family vacations, honeymoons…"

"All occasions where people take photos!"

"Yep. It was like a home away from home for a lot of folks in town. They worked there. They celebrated there. The annual Christmas Eve open house meant the world to my family after my dad died. It and our faith were our only constants in a world of chaos. That's why I have to have it ready for guests by that time this year."

"Oh, Andy." She tilted her head. He was not a man who shared that kind of information with just anyone, she could tell. Suddenly, his passion for getting the inn done and done right took on a new meaning. "You know you don't have to do the work on the inn all by yourself. You just saw your neighbors in town pull together for the park decorations. You should—"

"I should tell you about the town museum. It's right across from the park in City Hall, fourth floor."

"Not as subtle as bursting into song, but I get it. You want to change the subject." She moved from around the desk and crossed her arms. "I'll play along. Tell me about the town museum."

"Oh, you should really go see it for yourself." He reached for her coat and held it open for her to slide her arms in. "They have the whole history of the area, including a section just for the Snowy Eaves Inn. People have donated photos, scrapbooks, souvenirs. Those along with the town archives of newspapers, yearbooks and what have you, who knows? You might get a lead on finding your father."

She shrugged into her coat and glanced back at him, with her eyes narrowed. "You don't fool me, Andy McFarland. This is all part of your attempt to get me to formulate a plan."

He smiled slightly, wrapped her scarf around her neck then turned to retrieve his vest. "You can thank me later."

"I will. Maybe at the park lighting…you know the one you hadn't planned on attending," she teased as she opened the door and stepped back out into the brisk New England morning, leaving him speechless.

Chapter Five

The rest of the day went swiftly by. Or at least Corrie *realized* it had gone by when she found herself sitting alone at a library table in the silent fourth floor museum squinting to make out the faces in a faded instant photograph pasted into a scrapbook. "Mom?"

She skimmed her finger over the photo of a group of young people standing with gardening tools in front of what looked like a quaint little log cabin, then inched in close to try to make out the features. The light through the blinds on the row of large windows that looked out over the front of the building had already begun to fade. She looked up to the row of metal file cabinets on one side, then behind her to discover the dusty displays cloaked in long shadows. A quick check of her cell phone told her it was almost four o'clock.

She set her glasses aside to rub her eyes as she pressed her spine straight against the rigid back of the chair. After hours of sitting hunched over any piece of information she could find about the Snowy Eaves Inn or anyone in the area with the last name Wallace, the movement sent a warmth circulating through her muscles. She rolled her head to ease the ache in her neck.

If only she could dispel the ache in her heart with such a small effort.

How could she have worked so hard and literally come so far and still have nothing? She had no solution for the gingerbread inn, no lead on her father and no chance of snow in the forecast. "At least I have Andy."

A door creaked on the floor below.

"To help me, that is. At least I have Andy to help me, um, with the gingerbread contest and...all," she hurried to qualify, even though there was no one around to have heard her. She was alone. All alone.

She sighed. Probably just feeling a touch of homesickness, right? Her mother had probably felt the same way the summer she came to the Snowy Eaves Inn. She turned her attention to the photo, then to her cell phone.

Corrie pressed the first number on her speed dial, took a deep breath, then held the phone up to her ear. There wasn't anyone else around to overhear the conversation but putting it on speakerphone seemed too impersonal, too distant. She wanted to hear her mom's voice in her ear, to hold the object connecting them across all these miles, even if it was, at best a tenuous connection.

"Bennington's Bakery, Barbara speaking."

"Hi, Mom. You busy?"

"Not too busy for you, honey. Is anything wrong?"

"No. Not...wrong." Just hearing her mom's voice brightened Corrie's outlook. They had spoken during the drive up and last night when Corrie finally got settled in her room at Maple Leaf Manor but that had been dutiful daughter stuff, checking in, making sure her mother knew how to find her, that kind of thing. This call? "I just…I think I'm looking at a picture of you."

"You think? You don't know?"

Other mothers might have been curious or confused by a remark like that. Corrie's mom wanted clarity. She wanted to hear that Corrie was in control. "I'm at the town museum in Hadleyville, looking for information."

The muffled background sounds of the bakery filled the slow, steady passing of the seconds.

"On the inn," Corrie added after that prolonged moment of silence on her mother's part.

"And?"

Such a loaded question. Corrie could think of a dozen things she could throw out there. Some would mollify her mother. Some would mortify her. The truth? Corrie had no idea how her mom would respond to that, and that scared her more than any other possibility.

Yes, the girl that proudly embraced making things up as you went along wished with every fiber of her being that she knew exactly what her mom would do if she poured her heart out on the spot. Suddenly, she felt more alone than ever before. "And…there's a photograph in a scrapbook of a girl and two guys holding garden tools standing in front of what looks like a little log cabin. I think you might be the girl."

"Does this girl have dark hair, permed within an inch of insanity yanked up in a ponytail on one side of her head?"

Corrie smiled at the description. "Yes."

"It's me."

And? Corrie wanted to use her mother's own ploy to draw more information against her.

"Was that all you wanted to know?"

Corrie wanted to know if one of the boys in the photo was her father. "I just…there's no caption under it, no other information. I just thought maybe you could tell me more about it."

"I don't know what I can tell you without actually seeing the picture, honey. I know my mother hated my hair like that. She called it wild and worldly. When I came home after that summer she…" Her mother paused to clear her throat.

As rocky as Corrie and her mom's relationship had been, it seemed like a sunshine-dappled, lovey-dovey, mother-daughter picnic compared to the way Corrie's mom and grandmother had gotten along. It had gone from bad to worse when Barbara returned home expecting a baby fathered by a stranger that she never heard from again.

"After that summer she forbade me from wearing my hair like that again." Another throat clearing. A sigh. "Of course, thinking back on it now, it was such an awful style, in some ways I think she did me a favor."

Her mother had done the best she knew how to do, that's what Corrie's mom was saying. That was pretty much all Corrie was going to get and she knew it. She could ask about the boys, but her mom was right, without seeing them, how could she say for sure who they were. The photo was too old for her to snap with the phone on her camera and get a good likeness.

"Okay, Mom. I just wanted to hear your voice."

"It was lovely hearing from you, sweetie. I'm keeping you in my prayers."

"Thanks, Mom."

"Corrie, honey?"

"Yes?"

"I hope you find what you're looking for, but I can tell you, you won't find it in a museum, or an old photograph." Her mother's voice grew thin then rallied as she added, "Bye now. I love you. Knock their socks off at that contest."

Corrie whispered a goodbye to her mother then ended the call and set the phone aside. Another dead end. Clearly her mom did not think the man was to be found here. She closed the scrapbook, put her glasses on again then pushed up from the seat. She walked to the windows, her footsteps echoing in the large, lonely room.

She reached out and gave the old cord dangling beside the grayed Venetian blinds a yank. The metal slats clattered upward, unevenly. Late-afternoon light flooded the space. She leaned forward to rest the heels of her hands on the windowsill and looked out over the main street of Hadleyville, Vermont.

"Where are you, James Wallace?" She scanned the length from the park she had helped decorate this morning, to the shops and businesses all decked out with wreaths and lights. "One thing seems certain. I am not going to be able to find you on my own."

"You want to respect his privacy, but you can't find him without going public? You are in a fix."

"Andy!" The man's sudden appearance in the

doorway at the top of the stairwell made Corrie jump. "Why didn't you whistle while you came up the stairs or something? You scared the fire out of me."

"The fire out of you?" He laughed and crossed the room toward her, stopping at her side as he looked down into her face and said, "I very much doubt that. I have an idea you have plenty of fire left."

"If I do, I'll use it to scorch your hide if you ever make my heart race like that again."

"Me?" He pressed his work-roughened hand over the thick knit of his ivory-colored sweater. "I make your heart race?"

"By startling me," she clarified, even though under better circumstances—ones where he wasn't totally focused on work and family and she didn't live a thousand miles away—she might have confessed that every time she looked into this man's eyes, her pulse did quicken.

"Sorry." He made himself comfortable by half-leaning and half-sitting on the windowsill. The stiff denim of his clean, pressed jeans rasped as he stretched out his long legs and crossed his ankles. "I came back in town to get Greer from school and thought I'd drop in to see how the research was going. Not well, I take it?"

"Nope." She shook her head and pressed her fingertips to the cold glass of the window. "I've pretty much concluded that James Wallace wasn't a local guy."

"Don't give up that easily." He folded his arms and shifted his upper body until the light from the window shone on his handsome face. "You can still ask around town about him."

"I haven't quite figured out how to do that discreetly.

I mean, what if he has kids and a wife who don't know about me? That would be a rotten way to find out, because I went around asking people all over." She traced her finger down the glass then took a step backward. "I wish I could narrow it down some."

"Narrowing it down? Is that code for creating a plan?" He gave her a needling grin. "Why don't you just ask people if they know any families named Wallace. If they do, you can go to that family and ask if they know a James Wallace."

"That might work! Only I'm not sure how to do that with all the excitement of the lighting and all."

"Then ask before the lighting. How about over a meal?"

"A meal?" There was that heart racing thing again. She touched her chilly fingers to the base of her throat and when a strand of hair brushed her knuckles she tried her best to smooth it down to make it presentable enough for a dinner out on the town with Andy.

"Our church youth group is having a chili supper in the church basement before the lighting to raise money for their summer mission trip." He stood straight and gave a jerk of his head. "Come with me and you can ask folks there."

"Chili? Basement?" She laughed even though he had no way of knowing she felt silly and probably thought she was playing coy or something totally inappropriate. That only made her laugh more even as she said, way too brightly, "Sure. Great. What time?"

"Starts at five, but since this place is about to close, I just dropped Greer off over there and that's where I left my coat. We could head that way now."

"Okay." She lead the way toward the stairs but took a moment to stop and grab her coat and scarf. "So, you're a churchgoer?"

"I was raised in the church." He took the coat from her and held it for her to slip her arms in. "I still help out when my mom asks me to but, well, my life has gotten busy lately and…"

"Too busy for God?" she asked, turning slightly to help him help her into the bulky pink coat.

"Too busy for *church,*" he corrected with a stern note in his voice. That tone softened as he flipped up her collar, draped her scarf across the back of her neck and said, "Or more precisely, too busy for all the obligations that go with a small church in a small town."

She struggled with her buttons. "Oh."

He sidestepped around her and moved to the top of the stairs. "You sound like you're taking that personally."

"Maybe that's because I was one of the obligations taken on by a small church in a small town." She swept along to catch up with him. "I love my mom and she is a Christian, but she believes that people are pretty much on their own in the world."

She paused and looked up at him, giving him a chance to say something, though she wasn't sure what she expected him to say.

It wasn't until he just nodded and said nothing that it dawned on her what she had hoped to hear. A denial. She wanted to hear Andy say that people needed each other. That he needed…someone.

When it didn't happen, Corrie sighed and headed down the stairs. "Just after I pushed my mom to try to find my father and she couldn't, she tried to emphasize to me even more that I had to rely on myself in life."

"That's a lot for a little girl to have to carry."

"Thanks to my church, I *didn't* have to carry it." Their footsteps rang in the enclosed area. "They stepped in and sort of became my surrogate family. There are only a few members still at the church from that time but they were a lifeline to me then. Good thing none of them were too busy for church."

"I get your point." He hurried down to catch her on the last landing, snagged her gently by the arm. "But that hardly applies to—"

The first-floor door swung open and the mayor, Ellie Walker, stood at the threshold gazing up at them. She whipped off one pair of glasses and just as quickly replaced them with a second pair that had been dangling from a chain around her neck.

The sight of the woman, who was exactly as tall as Corrie but more than a little bit wider around, startled Corrie while at the same time putting her at ease. It had been that kind of day, after all, full of surprises and letdowns, a regular emotional roller coaster. Having the mayor pop in on them seemed the perfect topper to the afternoon.

"Oh! My! I didn't mean to intrude." The mayor smiled in a way that reminded Corrie of someone, a Cheshire cat maybe? "I was just going to come up and tell you that that we're about to start locking up the building."

"You're not intruding," Andy dropped his hold on her. "We were just talking about—"

"Family," Corrie rushed to rashly supply. She shot him a shy sidelong look in hopes that would let him know she regretted her remark about being too busy for church. It was not her place to say it. Nothing about Andy was her business and had nothing whatsoever to do with why she had come here. Family was why she had come and this was her chance to start asking about her father. "I guess you know just about every family in Hadleyville, don't you, Mayor?"

"Oh, not just Hadleyville." She held the door open for them to walk past her into the hallway of the main floor. "I grew up on the other side of Mt. Piney, in Daviston. I know families all over these parts."

Corrie stole a glance at Andy, who gave her a nod as if to say "go on, ask, I know you want to." For a guy who thought too much like her mother, he sure was the kind of person Corrie liked knowing had her back.

"So, would you happen to know any Wallaces?" she ventured.

"Only my nephew in Virginia, but if he knew that I told you his real first name was Wallace, he'd never speak to me again. Of course, right now he only speaks to me when he comes here for Christmas so I suppose I'm safe. Why do you ask?"

"That's the big question, isn't it? Why *do* I ask?" Clearly her mom didn't think she'd find her father. Corrie had no idea what she would say or do if she did find him. "I guess that's something I'm going to have to figure out if I ever hope to get any real answers."

Chapter Six

Corrie didn't get any better answers at the chili supper. Nobody knew any family with the last name of Wallace. All the while she went around meeting people and trying to work that into the conversation, Andy pushed up his sweater sleeves and dove in, setting up tables, corralling kids, even taking out the trash.

Corrie couldn't understand this man. He seemed so determined to do everything himself when it came to restoring the inn but never hesitated to be of service to others. On the surface it looked like such an honorable trait, but Corrie's experience told her that people who did not understand the importance of give *and* take could make life very hard on those who cared about them.

In such a short time Andy McFarland had done so much for her, she thought as she waited by the door for him to get Greer ready to go out into the cold night air. If Corrie could get Andy to accept a little help, he'd be so much happier. That's all she wanted to do, she justified, leave him a little happier when she went home to South Carolina. That's how she would thank him for helping her look for her dad and with the gingerbread inn. Yes, that's what she would do.

"Give and take." She smiled to herself.

"Did you say something?" Andy asked as he ushered Greer out the door past Corrie after they had eaten.

"I was just…coming up with a new plan."

"All right!" He held the door open for her. "Care to share it with me?"

"I'm, uh, still working on it," she said in all honesty as she walked outside and the cold air ruffled her hair and made the tip of her nose tingle. "Sometimes you have to see the way things might work together before you really know how to proceed, you know?"

"The way things work together?" He let the door fall shut with a thud.

"Or maybe how they *don't* work?" she ventured, knowing that wasn't quite what she meant, either. She laced her gloved fingers together. "Look, you're the big Mr. Fix it. Surely you've had to take a look at a project and come at it from a different angle from time to time. Take what you know works and what you think should work and compare it to what isn't working and—"

"I'm going to run ahead and get us a good spot," Greer announced. "Here, will you hold this for me, Corrie?" She pushed her school backpack into Corrie's hands even as she took off down the sidewalk.

"Walk, Greer. Don't push. Stay where I can see you," he called out as the young girl made her way to the park not half a block away. "Sorry." He turned to Corrie and motioned for her to walk with him. "She's all worked up."

"That's okay." She slung the backpack over one arm

along with her purse. "I wasn't saying anything important. Just thinking out loud."

"No, no. You made a lot of sense in your own special way. I think I get it. You're saying sometimes you have to figure out why something broke before you can restore it." He spoke with enthusiasm as they walked along, as though energized by the concept. "And I think that might be what I need to do with the gingerbread inn."

"Shh, you don't want anyone to hear you talking about your working with me on my contest entry." She put her finger to her lips then smiled slyly just to tweak his he-man let-me-do-it-my-way-and-it-will-all-be-fine-little-lady ego.

"Thanks." He looked down, shaking his head. "Let me just say, I have a couple ideas for stabilizing your project but, you know, it might work better if I could see it put together. I'm in restoration, after all. Maybe I'd do better working backward from a completed model, flaws and all."

"Oh my goodness, that's perfect!" He'd just handed her a terrific way to teach the man give and take and also to bolster her hopes of creating a respectable entry in the upcoming contest. She grabbed him by the arm and gave it a squeeze. "Thank you, you won't regret this."

"Regret?" Andy took her by the hand and turned her to face him. "What are you talk—"

"And here the two of you are again!" Ellie Walker approached them with her arms spread, her smile wide and her eyes sparkling with mischief. "Andy, you are either the world's best ambassador for our town or Corrie here is—"

"She's his girlfriend!" Greer shouted as she practically

flew across the open space of the park to the sidewalk where they stood.

"No!" Andy said it before Corrie could. "She's just…"

"…a friend," Corrie finished for him.

"Who's a girl." Greer folded her arms and rolled her eyes. "A *girlfriend.*"

Andy started to speak but before he could, a chorus began to sing on the steps of the bandstand/gazebo. The evening came alive around them. People shuffled forward, sheltering steaming cups of hot chocolate in their gloved and mittened hands. A group of small children all dressed in reds and greens began shaking sleigh bells.

No one seemed interested in Andy's explanation but that didn't keep him from moving in close to Corrie and saying, "That came off harsh."

"It's okay." She didn't meet his gaze. The man had made it clear he didn't want people to know about his advising her on the contest. She understood why he'd also not want them to believe the two of them were dating. Especially since she would probably go home in a few days and never return, leaving him looking like she'd dumped him. If Corrie really wanted to get through to Andy, she had to keep her distance from him.

The crowd began to press in to get a better view of the activities. Corrie followed suit, hoping it would bring an end to the embarrassing topic of her being Andy's girlfriend. Or rather of him so strenuously not wanting her to be his girlfriend, not even wanting anyone to think she was his girlfriend. Her cheeks grew hot. She folded her coat more tightly around her body and put some extra distance between herself and Andy, just for safe measure.

"You see, just before you showed up at the inn, Greer said a prayer that I'd get a girlfriend by Christmas." Andy maneuvered with her, keeping himself at her side.

The aroma of hot chocolate drifted across from the cups cradled in the hands of people pressing close around them.

"I think Greer praying that is sweet," Corrie told him.

"Sweet, but I don't want her to think that's the way prayer works." Again he pushed closer to make himself heard, bumping against Greer's backpack as he did. "That's why I had to make sure she knew you weren't my girlfriend."

"I know. I'm nobody's girlfriend," she said softly, not really angry or even hurt, just more than a little annoyed that he felt compelled to go and point it out again. That agitation was probably why she couldn't just keep her thoughts to herself. "And while I totally get your not wanting to give into Greer's equating prayer with a virtual wish list, I believe that God does answer prayers."

The caroling ended and the mayor took the microphone. She hushed the crowd with an upraised hand. "I'd like to welcome you all…"

Corrie couldn't concentrate on a single syllable, much less make sense of whole sentences with Andy moving in so close. A strand of her hair got swept up by the wooly softness of his coat's lapel. The bulky buttons pressed through the thickness of her coat into her back.

The mayor went on. "Fourteen years ago…"

Andy raised his voice to make himself heard to her ears alone above the mayor's speech. "Sure. I'm not disputing that God answers prayers. But not like that, right? You don't just send up an order and suddenly there's—"

"Corrie Bennington!"

People around them began to applaud.

"Corrie?" Ellie Walker beckoned her toward the bandstand. "Come on up here and press the button that turns on the light display you organized."

"Me?" Corrie gripped the straps of her purse and Greer's backpack.

A smattering of applause began to build around her.

"Yes, you! You didn't think I was praising the talent and good taste of my fellow committee folks, did you? Half of them didn't even vote for me last election. How clever could they be?" She laughed at her own joke. "We wanted to thank you for all your help today and let you know that as far as we're concerned you can stay here until—"

"Until it's time to take the decorations down again," a gruff old voice shouted out.

"That should come 'round March," shouted a second voice from the crowd.

More laughter.

Only for once in her life Corrie didn't feel like rushing in and joining the impromptu joking. She had just figured out what she wanted to do where Andy was concerned and that involved playing it low key so as not to embarrass him and make him shut down.

"Surely there's someone local who deserves it more

than I do." She retreated a step and bumped into Andy's broad chest.

"You're welcome to bring Andy up here with you." The mayor smiled like she was in on a secret as she motioned for both of them to come forward.

"She's not my girlfriend." Andy held his hands up as if he needed to prove he didn't have any claim on her.

"You really do not have to keep saying that," Corrie grumbled over her shoulder to him. Then she spoke up, intending for the mayor and everyone else to hear. "I just think that—"

"I'll do it!" Greer raised her hand and jumped up and down from one foot to the other.

"Great idea. Let Greer do it." Corrie nudged the child front and center.

No one would have the heart to say no to the adorable child whose mother was detained helping others create families. Off the hook. No more chances for anyone to make cracks about her being Andy's girlfriend or for him to deny it. This was the best way to keep her distance from Andy.

Greer rushed up the steps.

The crowd showed their approval with a new round of applause, some murmuring and appreciative laughter.

Greer soaked it up with a wave and a smile so bright Corrie forgot about the cold. Or maybe that was because Andy put his hand on her shoulder and leaned in to whisper, "Thank you for doing that. You can tell it means the world to her."

"And takes the focus off you and me," she whispered back.

"Corrie, I just wanted to—"

"Shh, everybody. This is it." Greer stuck the tip of her tongue out and pressed the big red button on the extension cord.

Every eye lifted to the wires and bulbs lining the gazebo.

Nothing. Darkness.

Greer tried it again and then again to no avail. "Hey, this thing doesn't work."

Corrie let the backpack and purse slide to the sidewalk as she rushed up to the child. "Sweetie, I've found that if things won't work the usual way then maybe you need to—"

"I can fix it." Andy took two long strides and in seconds both of them had their hands on the button, Greer between them.

"...try something new," Corrie murmured, her eyes locked in Andy's gaze, her face just inches from his.

"We have a connection." Mrs. Walker raised her arms to make a show of plugging two thick orange extension cords together. "Go for it!"

Greer hit the button again and thousands of tiny lights came on all at once like scads of twinkling stars just a few feet away from them. They lit Andy's face and shone in his eyes.

Corrie's heart didn't just beat faster, she knew in that instant what people meant when they said their heart leapt. Was this how her mother felt when she met her father? Or was it just a trick of the moment, the meeting of sentimentality, excitement, possibility and Christmas?

The crowd cheered.

Corrie decided that it didn't matter why or how this

had happened, she would be forever grateful for it. Years from now, even if she had to go away without ever having found her father, she would have a wonderful memory of this place to cherish.

"Isn't it pretty?" Greer asked in awe.

"Beautiful," Andy said softly, his eyes never leaving Corrie's.

Christmas or pretty lights, Corrie didn't want to overthink why she felt the way she did or allow herself to remember that it couldn't last. For just one moment, just one time in her life, she didn't want to have to think fast or make new plans or wonder if she was really alone in the world.

"It's perfect," she whispered.

"You guys aren't even looking at the lights!" Greer said so loudly that everyone in the park seemed to hear and burst out laughing.

Andy shut his eyes and groaned under his breath.

Corrie pulled up straight. She pushed her glasses up and fidgeted with the fringe on her scarf as she turned to address all those faces peering curiously at her. "I just want to let everyone here know—"

"You're not Andy's girlfriend," a fair number of the crowd filled in for her dutifully.

Corrie managed a laugh through a wincing smile. She had been going to say something about how she had fallen in love with this little town even after only being here twenty-four hours.

"Enough!" Andy took charge, waving people off as he reminded them, "We didn't come here to speculate we came here to celebrate. I say let's get back with the program."

The mayor called for everyone's attention. The choir launched into another song. People began to shuffle around to look at the lights and talk to one another. Greer ran up into the center of the bandstand and began to twirl around. Andy went after her.

Back with the program. Back on track. That's the way it would be when Corrie left. Andy would see to that, probably welcome it. Earlier today, alone in the museum, she feared she would always be alone. Now in a crowd she had that same feeling. She supposed it might seem silly that she would think she could make Andy open up to the idea of not just giving but accepting help.

She gathered her purse and Greer's backpack and slipped quietly away from the Christmas activities. Still, she couldn't help thinking that she was the best person of all to teach Andy that lesson. It was all she had to offer him.

She turned to catch him pretending to skate around the floor of the bandstand holding his little sister up just high enough to keep her feet off the floor. She thought of the conversation they'd had about loving the inn. She saw how the man felt about his family and community. He could not be that hard to reach, she just had to find the right time and place.

Chapter Seven

"Andy!"

Unsure if he had actually heard his name or dreamt it, Andy pried open one eye and searched the darkness of the room in the inn where he had been bunking down the last two months.

Nothing. Not a sound. No movement.

He groaned and pulled the blanket up over the T-shirt and sweatpants he slept in just in case he had to get up to take care of Greer or a problem in the building. He must have imagined hearing his name. He hoped that was the case because he hadn't gotten nearly enough sleep yet. Not after spending most of the early evening trying to find Corrie at the Christmas lighting party and wondering why she had left so early.

After the gathering broke up, he had taken Greer back to the inn but when they pulled into the drive and he'd seen she'd fallen asleep, he decided to turn around and drive back to Hadleyville. Corrie's car was at the Maple Leaf Manor all right. That didn't tell him why she had crept away from the festivities without so much as a goodbye.

Had he done something to hurt her? To embarrass her? Was she angry with him? Just as he had a few short hours ago, Andy began to drift off to sleep with these questions colliding in his mind.

"Andy!" He heard his name through his musings. Louder this time, but still hushed and hurried.

"What?" He opened both eyes and looked directly out the open door of the room, into the empty hallway. The light from his alarm clock stung his darkness-adjusted eyes as he checked the time. "It's five-thirty in the morning. If I'm imagining this, I want it to stop. If not, well, I still want it to stop. Do you hear me…"

"Andy!" This time a face appeared in the doorway. Two faces, actually, if you counted the sock monkey, Buddy, that Greer held clutched to her chest as she poked her head around the side of the doorway.

"Greer. It's Saturday. I don't have to get to work around here for a few more hours. Let me get some more sleep and I promise when I get up I'll make you the biggest bowl of sugary cereal you have ever seen."

"In a couple hours it will be too late." She disappeared into the hallway, leaving her sock monkey's limbs swinging against the door frame as the only evidence she had ever been there.

"Too late for what?" He scrunched his eyes shut and yawned.

"Too late to catch whoever is downstairs," she whispered as she peered in again.

"Greer, I have told you a hundred times that nobody—"

Clang. The sound of metal ringing against something hard rose from somewhere below, followed by a thump and a thud, a crash then a bump. Then silence.

Andy was out of bed so fast he dragged half the covers with him. They fell into a pile on the floor. He had to disentangle himself as he told his sister, "Get in here. Lock the door behind you. Get in the closet with my cell phone and if I don't give you an all-clear in three minutes, call the sheriff. You remember how to do that, right?"

His sister nodded solemnly and did as she was told.

Andy hesitated for only a moment, wondering if he should bother with putting on shoes. He decided against it. He wasn't actually afraid so much as concerned. More than likely, it was nothing, a bit of equipment not put away properly that had fallen. Maybe one of the workers had come in early to try to finish up a job. That happened sometimes since the guys didn't get paid until they had completed each week's assignment.

Or it could be an animal, a raccoon or even a stray dog that found a way in and began foraging for food. Still, he said a quick prayer that he wasn't about to surprise thieves rummaging through the place in hopes of stripping out the copper pipes, hauling off the appliances or making away with anything from the doors to the light bulbs.

As his bare feet hit the icy unfinished concrete floor in the lobby, he said a silent prayer that all would go well, then looked around for a length of pipe or a board to use as a weapon if it came to that.

A noise from the kitchen made him freeze. A smack. Followed by a slap. And right on the heels of that, a thwap! Each had its own distinct sound and none of them put him in mind of a burglary in progress. In fact, it sounded to him like—

"La-la-la… La-la-la… La-la-la-la-la-la…hey!"

"Corrie," he muttered under his breath as he picked up his pace, built up steam and hit the swinging kitchen door with his arm straight. "Hey yourself! What are you doing in my kitchen so early in the—"

Corrie gave out a startled scream as she spun around, sending the bowl of flour in her hands exploding outward in a big white cloud.

A cloud that landed right in Andy's face.

"…morning," Andy finished, spewing the gritty flour and other ingredients and wiping them from around his eyes. He supposed he should have seen that coming.

Corrie gasped and put the bowl aside, practically stumbling over herself to get to him. "I'm so sorry that happened but to be fair, you did scare the stuffing out of me."

"And what do you think you did to Greer? Coming out here at five-thirty in the morning." He reached for a towel and began cleaning himself up.

"You told me you needed to see the gingerbread inn put together to get a better idea how to fix the problems I've had with it." She spread her hands wide to show what she had been up to. "So I'm baking. I told you that I start early in the morning."

"Baking I understand. Getting an early start, totally get that. What I don't know is how you got in here?"

"Greer gave me her backpack to hold on to. She had a key hanging on the side." Corrie motioned to the familiar pink pack now lying on the floor in the corner of the kitchen. She began looking around, opened the broom closet and got out the broom. Within minutes, she was taking care of the spilled ingredients coating the floor. "I didn't think it would be a problem since we'd talked about me coming here to put the gingerbread inn together."

"We did?" He had to step lively to avoid the whisking bristles. He took a minute to grab the dustpan and laid it down for her to brush the debris into. "When?"

"At the park. Don't you remember?" She took the dustpan from him, emptied the contents then put the broom away. After washing her hands, she began moving around the kitchen with all the grace of an ice skater taking command of the rink. "You thought it might help you to fix the gingerbread inn if you saw the problems?"

He scratched the back of his neck and when he looked at his hand, there was flour under his nails. He didn't know whether to laugh or grumble. "I did say that. But I don't recall us scheduling this."

"Scheduling?" She laughed lightly. "I didn't know I had to schedule baking gingerbread."

"Baking gingerbread in *my* kitchen," he reminded her.

"I have to have the entry at the community center no later than Friday at five. I don't have time for elaborate plans and meetings, Andy." She went to the fridge, opened it and reached inside. She brought out some eggs, milk and butter and closed the door with a swing of her hips. "You know it's not all bad having me here in your kitchen so early, you know."

"Bad?" He went to the kitchen island, pulled out one of the two stools alongside it and sat.

Corrie never stopped moving, placing the carton of eggs down, flipping it open, getting down a clean bowl, taking up a whisk, looking in cabinets.

He couldn't take his eyes off her. Even in what had to be a pretty unfamiliar setting, she showed no hesitance in going for what she wanted, whether it be a frying pan or a solution for her gingerbread problem. And when her actions didn't bring the results she hoped for, it didn't even slow her down.

"Let me just get one of these," she said under her breath as she reached around him to pluck a measuring spoon off the island by his hand.

She brushed so close he caught a whiff of vanilla and spice. He didn't know if it was her shampoo or the aftereffect of her work in the kitchen this morning. Not that it mattered. She should always smell like something rich and sweet and natural, he decided. It fit her so. As did those red glasses, that big apron and even those cumbersome boots.

In this cozy space with the cold darkness of a winter morning beyond these walls he couldn't imagine anything bad about having her in this inn, in this kitchen, in his home. He opened his mouth to tell her just that but before he could get the words out, another sound startled them both.

"Is that a siren?" Corrie put everything down and went to the swinging door. When she pushed it open a piercing whine filled the room.

"Greer! I forgot to give her the all-clear!" Andy got up so fast the stool wobbled and almost tipped over. He and Corrie both dove for it, each catching it by the edge, his hand covering hers.

"All-clear?" she asked.

"We thought you were a burglar," he told her as he set the stool upright. Neither of them took their hands away. "I'm not used to having anyone in my place this early in the morning."

"So you had Greer call the law on me?" A smile broke slowly across her lovely face. "I hope you still don't consider me too much of a threat."

"I think I can handle whatever danger you might bring my way," he said softly.

The air practically crackled between them. Andy felt that he had to say more, but what? If he reminded her that there could never be anything between them it might hurt her feelings. Or it might hurt his if she laughed in his face at the very idea he ever had a shot with her. If he said what he really wanted to say—to tell her that in just the short time he'd known her she had gotten under his skin like no other woman he had ever met—her laughing in his face would not just hurt, it would kill him.

For the first time in a long time Andy didn't just lack a plan, he had no idea how to formulate one. Corrie Bennington had him that far off balance.

"Andy?"

"Hmm?"

"You better go talk to the sheriff. Then maybe reassure Greer that everything is okay. I'd go up to her but seeing an unfamiliar figure in the dark upstairs might terrify her. So you go. After that, why don't all of you meet me in the dining room?"

"The dining room?" He thought of the roughed-out room that still needed the drywall finished, painting and above all, a floor over the unimpressive concrete there now. "What will be in the dining room?"

"A surprise." She patted his cheek then stood up and waved both hands as if to shoo him away. "I told you it wouldn't be too bad having me here this early. Trust me. Let me do something for you to smooth things over with the sheriff and ease Greer's anxiety."

Trust her? He did. Let her fix things for *him?* "I don't need help smoothing things over with anyone, Corrie. I told you I can handle it. That doesn't mean I don't appreciate the offer."

"And?"

A pounding at the front door echoed through the nearly empty lobby and dining room. "Andy? Greer? Is everything all right in there?"

Andy resettled the stool, which clearly had been fine and didn't need further settling, and gave her a brisk nod. "I'll go take care of the sheriff and Greer."

"And after that, bring them into the dining room. If you feel the need to do something more, set up a table and get out enough flatware for four."

He wanted to question that but with the sheriff calling out his name, he couldn't spare the time.

"Everything looks secure from out here but no one is answering. I don't know if Greer just called on her own and Andy isn't even awake or if something is actually wrong." The sheriff's voice was heard then a crackle and a response Andy suspected was over a walkie-talkie. "If I don't get an answer in a couple seconds, I'll find a way in."

Andy reached the door before the man—who was only a couple years older than Andy—got too worked up.

"Hey, Jim," he told the mayor's son as he let him inside. "Thanks for getting here so fast and for not breaking the door down once you got here."

Jim Walker placed his walkie-talkie on the spot on his shoulder where it usually lay quiet. He tipped his hat back with one hand then laughed. "I did a quick survey of the grounds before I knocked. Besides your truck and a pint-sized hybrid with South Carolina tags, no vehicles on the grounds. No signs of forced entry. I figured Greer was overreacting."

Andy grimaced. "What did she say?"

He followed Andy into the lobby, and slipped his hat from his head and began unsnapping his leather jacket. "Well, she whispered for starters, and said, 'You have to come and bring the big guns. They got Andy already but I won't let 'em get me.'"

"Big guns?" Andy rested one hand on the banister and shook his head. "I have to talk to Mom about how much TV she's watching. I'm going to go upstairs and let the kid know it was just Corrie Bennington, you know the baker who helped your mom with the lights yesterday? She's making gingerbread in the kitchen. Sorry about that."

"No problem. While I'm out here, need anything else?"

"Actually, Corrie asked me to bring you and Greer with me into the dining room and set up a table. Got something in mind, I guess. She thinks she's being helpful."

"Well, then, let's let her play it out. No reason to be rude." He positioned his hat on the counter where guests would one day register then tossed his jacket next to it. He clapped his hands together and rubbed them enthusiastically as he said, "You go see to your sister, I'll get the table ready."

Andy hesitated. He had expected his friend, upon finding nothing out of order, would just go about his business. That he wanted to cooperate with Corrie's scheme without even knowing what it was because it was the nice thing to do, needled Andy. Why hadn't he thought of that? Why hadn't he been that gracious when Corrie asked him to go along with her?

Because he didn't need her help, he argued in his head. Why encourage that waste of effort and time when he had everything under control?

He couldn't help sighing at his own bullheadedness as he trudged upstairs to tend to Greer. It didn't take much, once he mentioned Corrie's name, to refocus the girl's energy. She wrapped herself in her robe and took off like it was daybreak on Christmas morning, insisting that Corrie would need her immediately.

Andy took the time to change out of the clothes he had slept in and into some fresh jeans and a work shirt. He washed his face and neck to get the last of the flour, then brushed his teeth and checked his email to make sure his mom hadn't sent any new information. He wasn't stalling, he told himself, or worse, pouting because he didn't want to surrender to Corrie's offer. He was just going about his business. Stick with the plan. She was the one intruding, after all. Doing things that weren't even necessary. Again, he knew that was pride talking, and when he got sick of hearing his lame justifications, he made his way down the stairs.

"Mmmm. What smells so good?" he called out when his foot hit the concrete floor and he turned toward the dining room across the way from the big, open lobby.

"Only a southern breakfast so good it will make you want to slap your mama," Corrie said as she lifted up a huge platter.

Greer gasped.

Corrie set the platter on the table in front of Jim Walker, who tipped his head to one side and narrowed his eyes to study her.

"That's just an expression, Greer, honey. A good southerner would never slap his mama." She smiled at the girl then noticed Jim staring at her and inched back a bit. "Have I got flour in my hair? Jelly on my clothes? Egg on my face?"

Jim shook his head and chuckled. "No, no. I'm sorry. It's just that there is something familiar about you."

"Me? Really?" She worked the knot of her apron free, slid it from her neck and hung it on the back of a chair before taking a seat. "Were you at the lighting last night, maybe you saw me there?"

"Oh, yeah." He shot Andy a discerning look, like he was having trouble making all the pieces fit. "That must be it. Last night and then to see you here a few hours later."

"I hope I don't have to remind you that we called you because it was a surprise to find Corrie here this early in the morning," Andy said. He hoped his tone came off protective to Corrie and maybe just a tiny bit menacing to Jim, just in case the guy was jumping to the wrong conclusion about what had gone on since the lighting.

"Yeah. Yeah. Of course," Jim blurted out. "I didn't mean to imply anything."

A puzzled look came over Greer's face and Corrie's expression looked a bit bewildered as well.

"Look, it's not like Corrie is going to stay here. She came by to use the kitchen and will be gone as soon as possible."

"By Friday at the latest," she chimed in before she raised a small bowl with a spoon in it and asked, "Who wants gravy on their biscuits?"

"Friday?" The legs of Andy's chair squawked over the hard, cold floor as he scooted it forcefully backward. "Friday is, like, a whole week."

"Five days, if you don't count today. Or Friday." The spoon in her hand, brimming with thick, steaming gravy, hovered over Andy's plate.

"I have a timetable, you know." Suddenly, he didn't feel like such a heel for not instantly bowing to this woman's seemingly benevolent offer of help. Benevolent? Yeah, benevolent like a bulldozer.

He gazed into her eyes, trying to figure out what she was up to. She must have taken that as a sign that he wanted gravy. Lots of gravy.

She began ladling it over the golden, fluffy biscuits she had already laid out on a plate for him.

At the table, Jim couldn't seem to shovel the meal in fast enough.

Greer was pushing broken bits of biscuits dripping with sweet-smelling amber honey into her mouth like it was popcorn and Andy and Corrie were an action-packed movie.

Andy didn't care. He felt hemmed in and at the same time completely outside his element. He found himself torn between how much he cared about Corrie and his drive to come to her rescue and the carefully laid plans he had made to get the inn ready by the Christmas Eve open house. Those plans had been more than a year in progress. Corrie had popped up uninvited, unexpected, uncontainable.

But hadn't he allotted Corrie enough of his time already? He'd told her how to brace the top half of her gingerbread inn. Sure, it didn't deal with the roof issues, and he didn't know until they put it together if his suggestions would work, but... "I have a 'to-do' list as long as my arm."

"And what a nice, strong arm it is." She patted his biceps. "I have my own list, you know. And none of it can get done if I have to stop and move my project around, maybe risk ruining it and having to start over. As for *your* list, if you would let me—"

"I have a plan. A deadline." It was less of a protest and more of a proclamation of the simple facts. "Any of this ringing a bell with you?"

"I'm not trying to become a guest at the inn. I'll only work here during daylight hours then go back to my groovy digs at the Maple Leaf Manor." She smiled.

He tried to smile at the reference to the seventies-era decor of the Maple Leaf but he couldn't quite manage it.

"I won't get in your way. I promise," she said softly. "You know how strongly I feel about people keeping their promises, especially at Christmas, especially in this inn."

He met her eyes. He almost expected her to start humming "The First Noel," the song from the treasured snow globe that Greer had broken. From anyone else it would have come off as manipulation by guilt.

"Please?"

From Corrie, it sounded like a plea from the heart. She was getting nowhere on the search for her father. She hadn't seen so much as a flake of snow. She couldn't go home without even managing an entry in the contest. She'd told him that first night that he was the only one who could help her with that.

"Andy?" she prodded softly. "What do you say? Can I borrow some kitchen space until Friday?"

That's what got him. The call to be her hero. Corrie needed a hero. She had no hope of accomplishing anything she had come to Vermont to do without one.

He took a bite of the biscuits drenched in gravy to buy himself some time. The dense, savory flavor of butter, salt and pepper, herbed sausage and a hot, perfectly baked biscuit flooded his mouth. He chewed and swallowed and without taking even a second more to plot the right move, he looked Corrie in the eyes and said, "Take the whole kitchen. I'll do whatever I can to make it work."

Chapter Eight

"That smells great." Andy came through the kitchen doors near mid-day just as Corrie slid the last pan of gingerbread out of the oven. He stopped to take a deep breath and asked, "When can I get a sample?"

The professional-style baking pan, one of four that she had hauled all the way from South Carolina, clattered as she settled it over the top of the stove. She waved her hand over the baked cut out that would eventually serve as the side of the inn. Unintentionally, her action sent the aroma of fresh, spicy gingerbread wafting throughout the baking-warmed room. "Believe me, you don't want anything I've got here."

"Yeah?" He moved in to peer over her shoulder, leaning in close. "It certainly looks—"

Corrie didn't realize just how close he was standing until she turned around and found her nose practically nuzzling his soft flannel shirt.

"Good," he said softly.

"Thank you," she murmured. At least she tried to

murmur. Her lips formed the words but she didn't seem to make a sound.

He held her gaze for a moment.

Her heart fluttered. He was close enough to kiss her.

In another time and under better circumstances, she couldn't think of anything she'd have liked more than that. To kiss Andy? Just the prospect that it could, maybe, one day happen made her lips tingle and her skin tighten into a million tiny goose bumps.

Actually, even knowing that nothing could come of it, Corrie wouldn't have stopped the man if he had closed the gap between them and put his lips to hers. She wouldn't have pushed him away. Well, not right away.

He pulled back. "No way can you convince me that something you've spent this much time on isn't any good."

"Oh, it's good all right." She cleared her throat and turned back to the gingerbread in the shallow pan. "Good and sturdy. Not exactly a term we'd use to sell baked goods back home."

"Oh?" he reached out as if he might steal one of the scrap cookie bits and pop it into his mouth.

She slapped his hand. "You really don't want to try that."

Andy leaned back against the counter which made him able to look at her face as he said, "I thought you said everything on this gingerbread contest entry had to be edible."

"Edible, yes. Tasty?" Still flustered from thinking of kissing him and him clearly not interested in doing so, she gave a one-shouldered shrug to let him draw his own conclusion. "They don't give points for that, so it's okay to fiddle with the recipe to get the best building material."

"Really?" He crouched down and ran his open hand over the largest of the multiple gingerbread cut outs. "Too bad we can't improvise like that in the renovation business."

That caught Corrie's attention. If she really wanted to show this man that he could turn loose of his control issues, she had to use every opportunity to point out options. "As long as you're not compromising quality or safety, I don't see why you can't use some basic ingenuity to improve on—"

"It smells like Christmas in here!" Greer burst into the room, her hair flying behind her in a thick, shining ponytail that kept bouncing even after the child came to a stop, shut her eyes, poked her nose in the air and took a deep, noisy breath. "Ahhhh. I think you should bake gingerbread every day, Corrie."

"She does bake every day, you goof." Andy gave her pony tail a tug to get the kid to stand still.

"Not gingerbread," Corrie said. "Definitely not this kind of gingerbread. If you want I could—"

"As long as I don't have to eat the yucky stuff." She crinkled up her nose, giggled then covered her mouth with both hands. "Mom made gingerbread people last year and we spent all day decorating them. It was so much fun. But when I ate one. Blech!"

"Maybe my mom was using your improvised recipe," Andy gave Corrie a wink. "I'd forgotten that, short stuff. But now that you bring it up, I didn't much care for those gingerbread cookies, either."

Corrie moved the gingerbread, baking parchment and all, on to a rack on the last empty space on the counter. "Well, if you didn't come in here for the gingerbread, why are you both in here?"

"Lunch." Greer rubbed her tummy.

"Is it that late already?" She'd lost all track of time. She understood that it was meant to be a commercial kitchen but if she had designed it, there would have been more windows than the three high, narrow ones on the side wall that a person couldn't even see out of. She found the lack of natural light disconcerting.

"No, it's not quite lunch time. We came to ask you if you have plans for lunch?" Andy put one hand on his sister's shoulder. "We thought maybe we'd grab a bite to eat over at the Mt. Piney Café on the highway. After that we could take the full tour of Mt. Piney, which would mean we'd cruise through the post office parking lot then shoot across the street to see if the minister put up a funny saying on the sign at the All Souls Community church. Once you'd recovered from all that excitement, we could come back and build us a gingerbread inn."

"I'd love to embrace the whole Mt. Piney experience, but even if we had a huge lunch and took the long way around the town we still couldn't come back and start work on the inn."

"But I thought the plan was—"

"To keep it here until Friday," she reminded him. "The gingerbread has to cure overnight to be stable enough for construction."

"Oh." He rubbed the shaggy auburn waves flipping over his collar. "It's just that I have this afternoon open."

"No work on the inn?"

"Drywallers are in this afternoon," he explained.

"Hooray for drywallers!" Greer peered at the pieces of the inn laid out to cool.

"Hooray?" Corrie looked to Andy to clarify.

"Drywall is one of the last steps. The guys have agreed to work today until it's done, even into the night. So now I have all this time and no gingerbread. None to eat. None to build with."

"Aww, poor baby. Maybe we could—"

"What's this?" Greer, on tiptoe, had a piece of the cardstock template for the gingerbread edifice.

"Greer! Put that down. Haven't you learned your lesson about not touching things?" Andy took two long strides and had Greer under the arms, lifting her away from the counter.

The action sent the neatly stacked pattern pieces spinning and sailing out on to the floor. Corrie followed their descent, bending at the knees with her hands spread and her head down.

Andy bent forward as well, taking Greer with him and effectively turning the child's noggin into a battering ram.

A noise between a thunk and bonk…a *thonk*… resounded through the huge kitchen. Corrie went staggering backward.

Greer let out a cry.

Andy set the child down and gave her forehead a quick examination. "No damage done."

"It hurts."

"It's fine," he assured her.

"Mom would kiss it." She drew her mouth up into an overplayed pout.

"Well, Mom's not…" He caught himself midreminder of the child's absent parent and looked up at Corrie. When his eyes met hers, she saw a man who wanted to protect his sister but wasn't sure what answer would do that.

She chewed her lower lip. It was the kind of small, seemingly insignificant moment that could define a person to anyone paying attention. If Andy insisted on doing things his way, not the way his mom would have done them, then Corrie would know her hopes of getting him to loosen up his thinking would probably be for nothing. On the other hand…

"Mom's not the only one whose kisses can make things all better," he concluded.

On the other hand there might just be hope for him yet.

He planted an over-the-top lip-smacking kiss on his sister's head.

She giggled and wriggled and pretended to wipe it away, then looked up and pointed. "Now Corrie."

"What?" Andy suddenly looked anything but open to loosening up. He held his hand out and shook his head. "No. I don't think that would be appropriate."

"Corrie got bumped, too." Greer pointed to her own forehead. "You kissed *my* head. Corrie is company and you shouldn't give something to me and not give it to company. Mom says."

He stared at his sister for a moment and a slow smile crept over his lips. He laughed softly then gave Corrie a resigned look. "She's right. Mom does say that. Where did you get thumped?"

"Uh...here, I guess." Corrie put her finger to a spot just above her temple.

Andy leaned in.

She braced herself for the same kind of comical, exaggerated smack-a-roo that he'd given his kid sister. So she was in no way prepared for the soft, sweet and all too fleeting kiss that Andy dropped on the spot where her head still throbbed slightly.

"There," Greer summed up with a head nod. "All better."

"All better," Corrie whispered as she pulled away. Her eyes met Andy's and time seemed to take a deep breath and hold it for just a moment. She blushed. "I better check on that gingerbread."

He looked away and cleared his throat. "Let's get this pattern picked up, Greer."

Corrie spun on her heel and began to test the gingerbread cooling on the countertop.

"Look around, kid. This can't be everything." Andy laid the handful of stiff paper pieces down.

Corrie looked from the gingerbread to the pattern. "No, that's it. That's all there is."

"Where are the buttresses?"

Corrie glanced at the pattern then at all the pieces she had baked, the same number she had made on her first test run, plus the extra load-bearing pieces that Andy had recommended. "The what-tresses?"

"A construction system that supports the roof?" He tented his fingers to demonstrate. "You have no idea what I'm talking about, do you?"

She shook her head.

"It will be easier to just show you. Let's go take a look at the attic."

"The attic?" Greer's head whipped around. She flung the pieces of paper she had gathered on to the counter. "I love the attic. Can I go, too?"

"Sure."

"C'mon, Corrie. Follow me." Greer shot out the door, leaving it swinging in her wake.

Andy took a step and caught the edge of the door in one hand. He turned, holding it open for Corrie, and motioned for her to come along.

She slipped off the bib apron she had on and in doing so, brushed against the spot Andy had just kissed. To forestall the heat she felt threatening to flood her face, she reached over and grabbed her cell phone then forced her thoughts to the reason Greer had suggested the kiss. "You did a nice thing stepping in to kiss your sister's hurt away without letting her dwell on your mom not being here. Are you worried about her being away so long?"

"Worried?" He seemed to consider that as she walked through the door past him. When he let it fall shut behind him and came beside her to show her the way, he had his answer, "No. I learned a long time ago, when she started making these trips all over, that I had to leave her well-being with the Lord. I won't pretend that I'm happy that the red tape on this particular trip has taken so long and the pinch it puts me in, having to take care of Greer while I'm under this last stretch of construction crunch. But that's about my timing, not God's."

He was talking about his mother. Still, as Corrie

tucked her cell phone into her pocket, she couldn't help thinking *her* demands on his time didn't help that time pinch one bit. Still, he was a grown man, bringing a lot of this on himself with his stubbornness. "If you feel overwhelmed, then ask for help."

"I took this on myself and I need to see it through on my own." He started up the steps without so much as a glance in her direction as he said, low and quietly, "Expecting other people to step in to help finish what I started? Not my way."

Corrie held her ground at the base of the stairs, her hand on the banister.

Halfway up the stairs, Andy turned to his left and finally seemed to realize she hadn't dutifully followed on his heels. He paused and looked back at her. "What?"

She put her fist on her hip and pressed her lips shut tight.

He looked heavenward, groaned out a sigh and came down again until he stood one step above her. "Something you want to say to me?"

"I hardly know where to start."

He almost smiled, then his expression went serious but not stern. "Start by walking up the stairs with me to the attic."

Corrie did not budge. "In other words, do it your way."

He did laugh at that. He looked so good when he laughed. His eyes lit. His broad shoulders tilted back. Just the hint of tiny lines fanned out from the corners of his eyes, highlighting their green color.

The sight caused a flutter in Corrie's stomach but she

refused to let it throw her off track. "What if *your* way isn't working, Andy?"

He leaned down, not in any threatening way, but as if he wanted to catch every word, every nuance as he asked, "If you have something to say, Corrie, just say it."

"I'm just saying that if your way isn't working, Andy, maybe it's time to ask—"

"Hey! Are you two kissing or something down there?" Greer's voice rang out from the hallway above them.

"No!" They both said at once.

"Then come on. I want to show Corrie the attic."

"This discussion is not over," she warned him with teasing in her tone she hoped let him know she wasn't angry or judgmental. After all, she only had his best interest at heart. She moved past him to join his sister in the hallway then up a narrow enclosed staircase. "Okay, Greer, what is so great about the attic that you can't wait to show...whoa!"

"This is something, isn't it?" Corrie had hardly stepped into the large, open space when Andy came through the door, right behind her. "I guess it's where the staff used to come to get away from the guests."

"It's like stepping into a secret, private world right over everyone's heads. You know the staff snuck away up here whenever they could. I wish..." Corrie recalled she had brought her phone, whipped it out and began taking pictures. Being an interior space it would never be a part of her contest entry but as the child of two staff members who probably spent time in this very place, she wanted a way to remember it.

As attics went, it was larger than any she had ever seen. It was all natural wood but not raw. It seemed to have a light varnish over it, giving it a warm, rich glow. On either end were octagonal windows. In each direction the high pitched roof was held up by beams and every so often a wedge-shaped structure between the roof and the floor. Each of those were covered with writing, carved and painted and written in permanent marker.

"It's like a record of all the people who have been here over the years. I wonder..." Corrie struggled to breathe deeply and keep her calm. Her phone's camera clicked as she recorded what she found. But after a minute, she stopped trying to catch every angle. She began to touch the names, initials and dates adorning the beams and buttresses, searching for some confirmation of her parents' time together at the Snowy Eaves Inn.

"You should see it at night!" Greer told her, pointing upward. "Especially when the moon is really bright."

"There are windows." Corrie turned, finding herself just inches from Andy who must have followed her as she had followed her curiosity deeper and deeper toward the end of the attic.

"Actually, they're skylights," he said, looking up, too. "I think they might have planned to make this a dormitory-style sleeping space but I don't think it ever got past the 'someday' stage."

Being stuck in the "someday" stage resonated with Corrie, especially standing so close to Andy in this place where her parents might well have made their own someday plans. While he studied the glass above them, she stole away, heading back toward the doorway, and checking the writing on the other beams and buttresses. "I wonder if it matters that I didn't put one of these in *my* inn."

"Sleeping space?" He stood there a minute, his hands on his hips, watching her.

"Skylight," she said quietly.

The earnest directness of his gaze made her self-conscious, but strangely, not in a bad way. She wondered how her hair looked with the winter sun filtering in through the skylights. If her glasses made her look quirky or kooky or geeky...and if Andy liked quirky or kooky or geeky. She wondered if he thought she looked like she belonged in his inn.

She turned toward him and placed her hand on one of the beams overhead as she asked, "Do you think that might be one reason why my roof slides? I mean, if I cut even small squares in the roof it would decrease the weight, right?"

"You may be on to something." He strode purposefully toward her, stopping under the same skylight as her. "Then you pair buttresses and beams?"

His nearness made it hard for her to concentrate, hard for her not to just stand there and stare like a goof and think how cute he was, how sure and confident. She clicked off a pic of him.

He sort of scowled and squinted, rubbing his eyes after the flash, "Why did you do that?"

Good question. She had come here with clear goals in mind, entering the contest, seeing snow, finding her father. Meeting a great guy and harboring a monster crush was not on the list.

"Got a picture of some initials." She twisted her wrist

to show him the photo she had captured of him and the ex-staff members' graffiti behind his head. She glanced at the picture herself. "Hey, BJ loves BB. BB—those are my mom's initials! If only that was a JW who loved BB, but still…" She flashed the photo his way again, glad for the distraction to cover for her actions. "Nice picture, huh?"

Corrie shut her eyes and tried not to groan out loud. She had come out to the inn this morning determined to nudge Andy away from his almost stifling need to stick to a plan and instead she ended up lecturing herself on keeping her eyes on the prize. She opened her eyes again and found it difficult not to think that she was looking at a pretty worthy prize right now. Not that she'd give up her other goals but why couldn't she add a sweet, brief Christmas romance to the list?

People learn best by example, after all. Maybe the best way to get through to Andy would be to, well, get through to Andy.

"I think this just might be your answer," he said softly as he lowered his gaze from the beam overhead to her face.

"I think you just might be right," she murmured as she moved into cozy closeness, laid her hand on his chest and tipped her head up in perfect position to be kissed.

"Corrie…" he brushed his knuckles over her cheek as he whispered, "Do you really think we should risk—"

"What answer? Where? I want to see." Greer pushed her way between them and craned her neck to look up. "Is it something somebody wrote?"

"No." Andy pulled his shoulders up and shifted his

boots to create distance between himself and Corrie. Then he coughed into his hand and frowned up at the nearest beam. "It's a structure thing. You have to get things in the right order before you can build on anything, Greer. That's the answer. First things first, get the foundation and framework down, you can't neglect that. It's a priority that you've got to stick to."

He spoke to his sister but he meant it as a message to Corrie. She tried to take it well. That, after all, also demonstrated her philosophy that rolling with what life hands you is better than being so rigid.

She took a step back and snapped three photos in a row of the beam over Andy's head, then she lowered the camera without even checking the screen to see what she had captured and sighed. "So much for that. I guess I really did get my answer. C'mon, Greer, let's get back to work in the kitchen."

Chapter Nine

Awkward. That was the only way Andy could describe the rest of the day in the house after that near miss of a kiss in the attic. As Corrie whipped up more dough and created the buttresses out of it, he had wandered in and out of the kitchen. He'd say he wanted to check on the progress of the gingerbread inn when he came in, then after a few strained minutes announce he needed to go and check the progress of the drywall in the real inn's dining room.

Why he couldn't just shrug it off and stay in the kitchen making small talk he didn't know. Why did it matter? Corrie was just a woman, after all. Just passing through. Not part of the plan. And yet, when he looked into her eyes, when she touched his arm or teased him about his commitment to his plans, it mattered.

He had contemplated that as he watched the workers putting up drywall. The old walls seemed perfectly straight at first glance. A quick and easy job requiring no special attention, the workmen thought they'd knock it out in no time. Then they got to work and found it almost impossible to get all the edges to meet up square and neat. They knew how to handle that, of course, but it meant they'd have to work longer, make some adjustments, change the plan.

Andy couldn't help comparing that to his relationship to Corrie. Two people with simple, straightforward goals who had special ties to this old inn, who seemed to both be headed in the right direction. To people like the mayor or Greer, even to Corrie herself, it might seem the two of them would make a great fit. But Andy believed that no matter how hard they tried to make it work, it could never quite come together.

He wasn't going to up and move to South Carolina. He certainly wouldn't expect Corrie to move here. And even if she found her father nearby and moved to the area, what then? With her reckless approach to life, he'd find himself perpetually running to her rescue, always playing her champion with a safety net. His mom and sister still needed him too much. His business needed him. He'd committed himself not just to do restoration work but once he'd completed work on the Snowy Eaves, he dreamed of running it. He had enough to take care of without taking on Corrie Bennington.

He had charted his course when he decided to restore and run this old inn and he had to stand by that.

Then why couldn't he get that girl off his mind? Even long after she had left that day, the smell of gingerbread in his kitchen kept tugging at the coattails of his concentration. Her face, her laughter, the way she pushed up those red glasses or clomped around in those big boots popped into his thoughts at the most inconvenient times.

It always caught him by surprise, just as she had done at the community decorating party and when she came blustering into his life on the winds of that rainstorm. He thought of her as he worked on the inn and as he got a snack from the kitchen. He thought of her that night as he tucked Greer into bed and she asked for a story. Andy drew a blank.

"I hadn't planned on you being out here this long, kid. We've read all the books you brought from home."

"Corrie would have known a story," Greer muttered.

"Or just made one up on the spot." His agreement came in more of a murmur than a mutter. "I bet it would have made you laugh, too."

Greer needed to laugh more, he thought at the time. But the next morning, as she went skipping off into her Sunday school room full of squealing kids in the church basement, he realized he'd been thinking of himself. He needed more laughter in his life. More fun. More than just work and worry. More…

He looked around at the caregivers and teachers and family members taking kids to the nursery, the classrooms and the gym where they held the worship and praise service for high school and college-age people. People talked all at once. They greeted one another with open arms and open hearts.

He needed more life in his life, Andy concluded and before he could try to imagine what that would look like—*who* that would look like—he hunched up his shoulders and scoffed.

He didn't have time for that right now. He had obligations. He had well-laid plans that needed his full focus. He couldn't afford the distraction of—

"A friendly face!" Corrie Bennington stood at the bottom of the stairs. "Am I ever glad to see you, Andy McFarland."

"And I'm…surprised to see you, Corrie."

"Yeah. I thought it would be okay if I skipped church this Sunday, being so far from home and all but then I woke up early this morning, all full of, well, energy. Wanting to get to work putting the inn together, ready to see how it would fit and if it would be like I dreamed it would be, you know?"

"Actually, yes, I do know that particular feeling." He nodded trying not to show how much it got to him to hear his own inclinations voiced by this woman who he couldn't get out of his mind.

"So I remembered this was your church and I thought, well, I'm awake and I want to go out to the inn when you're done with church so here I am." She held her hands up in a sign of surrender as a shy smile broke slowly over her lightly glossed lips.

"Here you are," he echoed softly.

"And here you are." She jabbed her finger toward him. "Coming to my rescue once again."

"Rescue?" *Red flag.* The word made him retreat physically, and emotionally.

"I kind of got turned around in this big ol' church. Ended up in the gym." She crinkled her nose not in distaste but sort of self-deprecating. "I think I'm a little mature for that crowd."

"I think you'd fit in wherever you go." He relaxed again and put his hand on her back to gently guide her into turning around and heading up the stairway. "But I understand what you're saying. The main sanctuary is this way. The service starts in about ten minutes."

As soon as they were headed in the right direction he could have let his hand drop from her back. But he didn't. He told himself he was just being a good host, making sure she didn't lose track of him in the bustle of churchgoers. Except that most of the churchgoers in this sleepy New England town were decidedly unbustling in their approach to worship. And if he had lost direct contact with her, he'd still have been able to pick her out amidst the rest of the congregation in her bright green sweater, white wool skirt, clunky boots, velvet headband with a sprig of fresh holly pinned to it and those red glasses framing her beautiful, sparkling eyes.

"Do you have a certain pew where you like to sit?" She turned slightly to ask him over her shoulder.

"I, uh…" He checked the clock in the lobby and winced slightly. The spot near the back by the door where he could slip in and out unnoticed had probably already been claimed by some other unmarried guy trying to stay out of the spotlight of well-meaning mamas with single daughters. "Why don't we just go in and see what we can find?"

"Sounds like a plan." She raised her eyebrows and her lips twitched in a hint of a smile at his having to take her approach and improvise. She accepted a bulletin from the greeter and took a step toward the door of the sanctuary.

With that she moved from the shelter of his touch. It didn't seem to register with her but it made Andy's hand feel suddenly cool and empty. Just the way, he suspected, his life would feel when Corrie Bennington left town for good in a few days.

He took a deep breath and tried to shrug it off only to find a big hand clamped down on his own shoulder.

"With that pretty little girl again, I see," said the gruff, familiar voice of Larry Walker, the mayor's husband. "First at the decorating party, then the lighting ceremony. Now church on Sunday. Have to say, son, for a fellow who's avoided the big romantic-type commitments for as long as any a man can, when you fell, you fell hard."

"Fell?" A quick punch in the stomach better described how the man's assessment felt to Andy. "I haven't… I didn't…"

Larry worked his way on by and made his way to his usual spot with the other elders of the church on the second row.

"Didn't what?" Corrie asked as she smiled to Larry and led the way to the first open pew a few rows away.

"Fall," Andy said softly, watching her slip so easily into his church, his community and, if Larry was right, into Andy's heart.

Andy tried not to think too much about that as the bell choir did a performance of "The First Noel" that made Corrie's expression move from melancholy, probably thinking of the broken snow globe, to a warm delight. While he didn't have any trouble concentrating on the message of the sermon, he felt some relief that instead of hymns that would require him to stand close enough to share a hymnal with Corrie, they sang Christmas-themed songs that he knew without music.

Afterward, he hustled her out of the sanctuary.

"Can't stop to talk." He waved off someone approaching them and pointed Corrie toward the stairway to get Greer. "Got an inn to build."

"Which inn?" she asked. "Yours or mine?"

"Both," he said to remind himself as much as her that he had other obligations beyond baking and decorating. He had this one day for that and no more. They had to make the best use of their time. "So, what's the game plan?"

"We're going to play a game?" Greer came winging around the edge of the open doorway, her smile beaming, with her black shoes and a bright red piece of paper in her hand.

"That's just an expression." Andy plucked the shoes from the child's small hands. The black flats slapped against the cold, hard floor as he plopped them down in a silent command for the kid to put them on so they could get going. "There is no game. There is no plan." He turned to Corrie to prod her to give him an answer. "At least not yet."

She shot him a sweet but slightly smug smile then turned to Greer and bent to tell her, "Your brother is trying to nudge me into getting my entry done as soon as possible so he can get it—and *me*—out of his kitchen."

Andy did not deny it. Just being honest, he thought, but when he saw disappointment flicker in those eyes behind those flashy red frames, he felt like a real jerk. To cover that, he switched his focus. "Whatcha got there, kid?"

"Something about the Christmas pageant." She

flapped the red paper as she balanced on one foot and then the other as she slid her feet into her shoes.

"A Christmas pageant!" Corrie tried to snatch the page but every time she got close Greer bobbled and it fluttered away. "Are you going to be in it?"

"Uh-huh." Feet firmly planted, she looked and pointed toward her coat hanging on a row of hooks on the wall. "It's on Wednesday and I'm going to be a Sarah."

Andy retrieved the small coat and held it out to his sister.

"A...a Sarah? I don't recall that name as part of the nativity story." Corrie finally managed to nab Greer by the wrist. She took the paper and tucked it in Greer's coat pocket as the two of them double-teamed the squirming eight year old to get her into her winter gear.

"Sure you do. Sarah Finn. The one who said..." Greer wriggled free and headed for the steps, calling behind her as she did, "Behold I bring you good tidings of great joy which will be unto all people!"

"Oh! A seraphim." Corrie laughed, gave Andy a wink then swung her arm out to take Greer by the hand. "You did that line very well, by the way."

"Thank you." Greer and Corrie climbed the stairs side by side leaving Andy to trail behind. "You have to be at least eight to have a line."

He considered moving in and just picking his sister up. Just to hurry things along, not because he didn't want Greer to get too comfy with, too dependent on Corrie. Again, he wondered just who he was shielding with those kinds of inclinations.

Surely not himself. He was the guy everyone else depended on. He was the guy who at not quite nineteen had single-handedly kept his family from losing everything after his father's death.

He paused on the steps for a moment making other families jostle him in their rush to get past. He hadn't thought of the struggle after his father's death in years. Why now? Because Corrie Bennington brought it out in him. She made him think about the way people depended on each other. About how, no matter how much you loved someone or how well your intentions, the person you trusted the most in the world could let you down, without even meaning to, because they didn't think ahead.

Corrie and Greer disappeared around the corner in the stairwell but Greer's excited words carried downward to him. "Andy helped me memorize my part so my mom would be proud of me when she gets home to see me in the play."

A punch to the stomach would have had less impact on him. He took the steps two at a time, in order to reach them. He liked Corrie but it was Andy's job to watch over Greer. He couldn't leave that responsibility to just anyone.

"That's great. But you know, if your mom can't get here by then, let's make a pinkie promise that you won't forget your line so you can do the whole thing for her when she does get home." Corrie said it with such kindness and enthusiasm that it made Greer clap her hands with joy. Corrie glanced behind her and smiled. "You promise to help her do that, Andy?"

"I promise." He exhaled and chuckled softly. Corrie wasn't just anyone. He looked at the woman, then at his sister. "I promise to help you do that, Greer, even if I have to play every other role myself."

Chapter Ten

"Do the donkey sound again!" Greer squirmed on a stool pulled up to the island in the inn's spacious kitchen.

Andy lowered his head. His shoulders lifted and then fell. He groaned. Then he seemed to reach down into the depths of what Corrie decided was the place where his good-guy-who-always-tries-to-put-things-right-and-doesn't-want-anyone-to-see-him-look-silly met his adoring big-brotherness. He lifted his head as he let out a comical "Eee-yaw! Eee-yaw!"

Greer clapped her hands and giggled.

Corrie couldn't help laughing, too. She also couldn't fight back feeling touched by the sweetness of a tough guy like Andy so willing to prove he could help his little sister reenact the nativity play. She pressed her lips together. Since the first time she had walked into this inn her emotions had gone round and round in an amazing mix of joy, anxiety and nostalgia for things she'd never known.

And hope. Hope for snow. Hope for finding her father. Hope for finding her own way. Hope for…

She didn't even know what she hoped for, only that seeing Andy like this made her want that elusive unnamed thing more than anything she'd ever hoped for before.

Andy laughed and gave Greer a hug. His gaze flicked up and his eyes met Corrie's.

Her breath stopped. She thought she smiled. Maybe she twitched. She knew she blushed by the rush of heat she felt in her face. Flustered, she spun around to hunch over her work to place the last piece of the gingerbread roof in place. "Well, you've done it again, Andy."

"What?"

"Come to my rescue." She stood back to reveal the basic form of the inn held together with thick white royal icing. "Your modifications made all the difference. Everything fits and so far nothing has buckled, slid, collapsed or tilted. Everything is just where it's supposed to be."

"Feels that way, doesn't it?" he murmured in a way that made her turn her head to meet his gaze.

Her breath caught in the back of her throat to catch him looking not at the newly constructed inn, but directly at her.

"When do we start decorating?" Greer hopped down off her stool and came close to peer at the inn. She stuck out the tip of her tongue and reached her hand out slowly.

"What's this 'we' short stuff?" Andy intercepted her before she could touch the inn by looping his arm around her midsection.

"First things first. We have to make sure it holds together before I start with the fondant, marshmallows, coconut flakes and all that other stuff."

"Wow, fondant? Marshmallows? Coconut flakes? Other stuff?" Greer's eyes seemed to grow bigger with every addition she imagined. "What's fondant?"

"In this case it's quick mix of marshmallows and water and lard that's going to make a kind of…" She rubbed her fingers together, then flexed them into fists, then held them up in surrender. "I'll make extra so you can have some to play with."

"All right!" The child crouched as if ready to launch herself upward in a great burst of unleashed energy.

Andy lifted his sister up and back. She squirmed, more as if she wanted to get a better look at the unadorned inn than to make an escape. Her legs began to swing and her small feet kicked slightly. "I think your inn stands a better chance of holding together if it doesn't have to share the same space as my little sister here."

Corrie wiped her hands on the corner of her apron. "Is that your way of suggesting I get it out of here as soon as possible?"

"Just the opposite. Suggesting I should get a certain somebody out of here as soon as possible."

"I know who you're talking about." Greer jabbed her thumb into her chest. "And I only wanted to help decorate."

Andy settled her on the floor again and she rushed up to the counter to look longingly at the basic structure of the contest-entry inn.

"It's no fair." Greer raised her eyes from counter level

to Andy then to Corrie. "I haven't gotten to decorate *anything* this year. Not even a Christmas tree. Dumb ol' renovations. Dumb ol' inn."

Corrie looked up at Andy and without saying a word as much as demanded he explain why that was.

"The place is such a… I don't even know where I'd put…" He ran his hand back through his hair. "There hasn't been any time."

Corrie stole a sidelong glance at her drying inn then folded her arms over her chest and lifted her chin to challenge the man's excuses. "There's time now."

"Yes!" Greer's little fist shot up in the air. She started to jump, but caught herself and just did a little wiggle instead.

Corrie laughed. "And as someone who has spent the better part of the last couple months thinking about decking the halls of this inn, I have a few ideas where to put a Christmas tree."

"We're getting a tree! We're getting a tree! Andy promised me when I came out here that we would!" Greer's wiggle turned into a jiggle then into a dance that had her hopping on one foot then the other across the tile floor. Halfway to the door, she spun around and nailed her brother with a guarded glare. "We *are* getting a tree, aren't we, Andy?"

He clenched his jaw. His brow furrowed.

Corrie held her breath.

"Ple-e-ease?" Greer begged.

Ple-e-ease? Corrie wished under her breath. Yes, she wanted Greer to have her tree but if that came with a chance for Andy to see that sometimes not going according to the plan was its own reward, well, Corrie liked that, too.

Andy's eyes shifted from his sister to Corrie to his sister again. Finally, he exhaled and chuckled at the same time. He bent his head and shook it. "Okay. You got me. A Christmas tree it is."

Greer clapped her hands and ran out the swinging door.

"Wear gloves and a hat, not just a coat," Andy called out after the child as he went to the back of the large kitchen and opened the door to the utility closet.

Corrie left him to get his own coat as she checked the royal icing joints of the gingerbread inn. "Great. I can grab my purse and coat on the way to the…"

She raised her head, suddenly aware of Andy standing in the doorway of the closet in his flannel shirt with a bona fide wood-handled, steel-bladed ax slung up on his shoulder.

"…car," she said in something of a squeak.

"What car? It's just a short walk out into the woods from here." He held his hand out to urge her toward the door that had just stopped swinging from Greer having pushed through it.

Corrie almost didn't trust her legs to carry her through that door. Still, she obeyed his request, disheartened to turn away from Andy looking all strong, manly and outdoorsy.

"So, we're really going to cut down our own tree, just like you promised, Andy?" Greer spun around in the open lobby space.

"Sure." He set the ax down long enough to slip into his coat and gloves, careful to keep himself between the dangerous tool and the excited young girl flitting around the room. "What's the point of owning all this pine-covered prime Vermont real estate if you can't get one measly Christmas tree out of it?"

A tiny thrill trembled in Corrie's stomach. "I used to shake up my little snow globe and dream of the Snowy Eaves Inn at Christmas time and now I'm actually going out on to Mt. Piney to help cut down a Christmas tree."

The light in Andy's expression darkened for a moment at the mention of the broken snow globe. "Corrie, I want you to know—"

"Are you going to stand here talking or go get our tree?" She didn't want anything to put a damper on this special afternoon. She slid her arm into the sleeve of her coat even as she threw open the front door. A blast of frosty air whooshed into her face, stealing away her breath.

"Brrr." Andy pulled a knit cap out of his coat pocket. "It's gotten a lot colder since church. Maybe we'll get some snow."

"No kidding?" Corrie couldn't help laughing out loud at the prospect, whirling around and throwing her arms around Andy's neck. "Thank you. Thank you. Thank you."

"For what?" He staggered backward, laughing.

"For letting me work on my contest entry out here." The brisk wind picked up her hair and sent it across her eyes and lips. She batted it away to no avail. "For helping me. For taking me along to cut down the Christmas tree. For...for...for snow!"

"I don't make the snow," he reminded her as he

brushed her hair back then took his own knit hat and fit it perfect on her head, rolling it up and back to accommodate her glasses. "And I can't promise we will get any today."

"I don't care." She didn't know if it was the cap or the company but she suddenly felt warm through her entire being. "Just having this moment to hope for it is enough. Just the possibility of something amazing makes it all worthwhile, you know what I mean?"

"Yes, Corrie. I do know," he said softly.

They stood there looking into each other's eyes, saying nothing.

She opened her mouth to say something, but she couldn't think of anything that she felt sure she wouldn't regret. She'd lived her life in the shadow of her mother's regrets and she knew it wasn't any way to make a full, happy life.

"Of course, possibilities are a little like weather predictions. No promise anything will come of them." He moved closer, holding her by her shoulders. "That's my way of saying—"

"I don't expect anything, Andy. Let's just enjoy this day. This one day. The problems with the inn and my family will all be there for us tomorrow. Let's have this day."

"Okay." He nodded.

She thought he might kiss her, but instead he adjusted the cap on her head, gave her a smile then bowed slightly his arm extended. "I give you this day, Corrie."

She had never had a gift as wonderful as that afternoon. The three of them went out, sometimes trudging, sometimes Greer and Corrie practically skipping along.

Deeper and deeper into the unspoiled, silent woods they went. Corrie had never seen anything like it or known any man like Andy.

He pointed out a prickly fir tree that barely came up to his chest.

Greer kept walking right on past him without even looking at it.

"I thought the goal here was to get a tree," he called after her.

The little girl glowered at him as only very determined little girls who know they have their big brothers wrapped around their fingers can glower. She crossed her arms and stomped her foot and without a word told him to quit fooling around and find her a proper Christmas tree.

He laughed and jerked his head to coax Corrie into following along.

Corrie took in the smell of damp earth and pine and the lingering hint of gingerbread that clung to her clothes and hair. She wrapped her coat around her. They had long ago lost sight of the inn. She felt as if the rest of the world had fallen away. It was only the three of them, the woods and the Lord.

This was the closest she'd ever had to having the family of her dreams.

Her heart soared. This was Christmas, she decided. To be with people you cared about. To know you could rely on them, no matter how many people had let you down in the past. To believe in the baby born in the manger and the seraphim who sang of joy and peace on earth. Corrie looked toward the paper-white sky and mouthed her gratitude to the God who had brought her this far, who had sustained her and gave her hope. "Thank you."

"That's it! That's it! That's the perfect Christmas tree!" Twigs snapped as Greer scrambled to get to a nearly seven-foot pine with full, green branches.

Andy gave the tree a once-over, checking for nests or any other issues that might cause problems later. When it passed inspection, he wrapped his strong hands around the ax handle and told the girls to stand back.

A crack rang out through the stillness of the winter day.

Corrie flinched at the sound but couldn't take her eyes off the sight of Andy, his muscles flexed and his expression intent.

Another blow reverberated through the crisp, cold air. The trunk of the tree creaked. One last whoosh of the blade, a splintering of wood and the tree fell with a muted thud.

"Yea!" Greer rushed up and patted the limbs as though stroking the fur of a pet cat. "It's so pretty. Now we just need to get it home and decorate it."

"Decorate?" Andy froze halfway down to picking up the tree at the trunk. "I don't have any ornaments out at the inn."

"No biggie." Corrie swooped down to take up the trunk of the tree to help Andy where she could. She gave it a tug and a twist, got the branches lying the right way and began to drag the tree back the way they had come. "You gave me this day. There's not a lot of it left, but I know what's in your pantry. You've got popcorn to pop and string and before I leave this evening, I can make sugar cookies to hang on the tree."

"That could work," he said as he snagged the ax, rested it on one shoulder then hurried up to take the top of the evergreen in his gloved hand to help Corrie carry it. "I'm sorry I didn't plan better, Greer."

"That's okay, Andy," the child said as she hurried ahead of them. "If things don't work out the way you planned, then you can always just make other plans."

Corrie shot Andy a look, trying not to grin too big as she said, "Well, at least I'm making an impression on one McFarland."

Chapter Eleven

They got the tree back to the inn and Corrie quickly helped them warm up with some hot chocolate. While they drank that, she laid out the directions for gathering ornaments.

"I can make some sugar cookies to hang on the tree. Nothing fancy, but I can use a glass to make circles and cut out diamonds and crosses with a butter knife." She narrowed her eyes and let the steamy aroma of chocolate warm her nose as she tried to imagine how to improvise for Greer's sake. "Oh, and I left those clear twinkle lights with the green cord from the park lighting in your truck, so we have those."

Andy hustled up a pencil and paper and had begun taking notes.

Notes! For impromptu decorating of a Christmas tree. She didn't know whether to laugh or grind her teeth in frustration. Or there was a third choice. She reached over and snatched away the pad of plain white paper. "Thank you, Andy. This is perfect. We can use this paper to cut out snowflakes to hang all over the branches."

"Hey!" He poked the pencil behind one ear and cupped his hot chocolate in both hands and grumbled with a hint of a smile, "I was making a list of what I need to do to get this whole tree thing organized."

"Trees do not need organizing." Corrie slapped the pad on to the counter. "One of my favorite lessons from the Bible is Matthew 12:26—Look at the birds of the air; they do not sow or reap or store away in barns, and yet your heavenly Father feeds them. Are you not much more valuable than they?"

"Yeah. God has it covered, Andy. You don't have to do everything." Greer downed the last of her drink, set the mug down with a solid thud then wiped her mouth with the sleeve of her bright pink shirt. "*You* gotta make the popcorn."

"All right, all right." He held his hands up in surrender and got up from his stool. "But while I do that, you need to go up to my room and get the little sewing kit on top of my dresser so we can string the popcorn once I've popped it."

She scooted out, leaving them alone.

"I, uh, I didn't mean to lecture you in front of your sister." Corrie had been so caught up in her own agenda she hadn't considered how she might sound reciting chapter and verse until just now.

"It's okay." He went to the cabinet and opened it. For a second he didn't get the popcorn out, though.

"Second thoughts on that? Something you want to ask me?"

"Actually, there is." At last he got down a big box from the overhead cabinet, turned and held it up for her to see. "Do you think it's cheating to use microwave popcorn on an old-fashioned tree?"

"No." She laughed and shook her head. "I say, take what's handed you and make the best of it."

"That should be your motto." He opened the cellophane wrapper, got out the bag, unfolded it and placed it in the brand new microwave oven. It seemed as if this simple task took every last ounce of his concentration until he punched the button and finally faced her to say, "That is, for the last few days you've certainly made things a whole lot better around town, around the inn, for Greer and for me."

"Really?" she whispered. Nobody had ever said anything like that to her before. Her whole life she had figured her very existence had made her mother's life worse. She tried to change that but she couldn't change having been born or that her mother had become a person determined not to rely on anyone else, ever. She had worried Andy was like that, now she knew differently.

It didn't alter the reality of their relationship but it still made her heart soar. Andy had not just given her this day, he had given her a moment that she would carry with her for a lifetime. "I've enjoyed being here. I've enjoyed…my day."

"Yeah, but what has it gotten you, really?" He stared at the window in the microwave oven.

The kernels began to pop, a few at first then more and more bursting in the bag louder and faster.

That's how her heart felt. She wanted to tell him exactly what she had gotten by coming here. A glimpse at what it meant to be a part of a family. Meeting a man who wanted what was best for others, not one who put himself first. A day. A moment. She didn't need anything else. She wanted to tell him all that.

"You still aren't any closer to finding your father." Andy cast his gaze down and rapped his knuckles on the countertop. "I feel bad that your helping us is taking time away from that."

Ding. The microwave stopped. Andy took the bag out and tore it open.

Corrie snatched up a big bowl she had used earlier to mix the gingerbread in and offered it to him. "It's taken my mind off hitting one dead end after another. Besides, finding my father was the dream. The real goal was to enter the contest and maybe see a real snow, you know, the kind that fills the sky and you can make snowballs with. Not just a dusting."

"You came all this way." The aroma of hot salty popcorn flooded her senses as Andy gave an ironic chuckle. "And we don't even have the good manners to have a decent snowfall."

"I still have a few days left until the contest, you know," she reminded him. She pressed her thumbnail into a seam made with royal icing to see how it was setting up. "You don't mind if I set my project aside and work on it tomorrow, do you?"

He put another bag of popcorn in. "Just as long as you stay out of the way of the painters."

"Painters?"

"They dropped off the paint for the dining room Friday afternoon but, of course, they couldn't start because the drywall wasn't finished. They promised to get started first thing tomorrow, but they're already a day behind schedule."

"What color are you using for the dining room?"

"Powder blue."

"Blue? Really?"

"Something wrong?"

"Sort of cold, isn't it?"

"There's a big fireplace in there."

"Not cold temperature cold, ambiance cold."

"Well, there are no color photos from when it opened sixty years ago but I asked around. The general consensus was powder blue."

"Fair enough. You can always warm it up with a good choice in drapes and tablecloths."

"Drapes? Tablecloths?"

"You hadn't thought of those, had you?"

"One more thing to add to my list. Right now I have to get the painters in and out, which will take a couple of days. I only hope the floors arrive on time so we can install them, then to get the trim work up. After that, if it's not already too late, I can think about drapes and tablecloths."

She would have gladly volunteered to take on that task if she thought for one minute she'd still be in Vermont by the time the work on the inn was done. Christmas Eve? She'd be back in South Carolina, back at the bakery, back in the life she had always known.

Corrie sighed.

The microwave dinged.

Andy took the second bag out and motioned to the door with a tip of his head. "I think it's safest if we take this out into the lobby."

He could have been talking about protecting the gingerbread inn from Greer. Or that the light in the lobby was better so that it would be better for working with a needle and thread. But when Corrie agreed with the man she had so wanted to kiss her in the woods, she couldn't help thinking it was the safety of their hearts he was referring to.

Again her thoughts went to her mother and the life lessons she had tried to impress on Corrie. No one can be fully trusted. You will always be let down. In the end you only have yourself to rely upon.

Corrie tried to repeat the worldly wise counsel over and over as she walked from the warmth of the cozy kitchen. But when she brushed against Andy's shirt-sleeve, looked up and met his eyes, the memory of his voice drowned out a lifetime of warnings. *You make the best of everything.*

Corrie strode into the lobby with a light heart only to find Greer standing there with her sock monkey tucked under one arm and her lower lip pushed out in an unmistakable pout.

"What now?" Andy wanted to know as he came up to his sister and bent down, his hands on his knees to meet her eye to eye.

"It looked so much bigger outside." She pointed to the tree.

Corrie stood back and took a long look. "She's right, you know. That wall of windows does sort of dwarf the poor thing."

Andy scratched his jaw and frowned. "What if I drag one of the smallest tables in from the dining room and we put it up on that?"

"I'll help," Greer said to show her approval.

"If we do that we ought to have a tree skirt, or a reasonable substitute." Corrie took a peek at the trunk in the cobbled together wooden stand he'd made for it earlier today. "You wouldn't happen to have a spare sheet would you?"

"Ah!" He held one finger up, and gave a comically maniacal grin. "I may have messed up on the drapes and tablecloths but I more than made up for it on sheets."

Greer giggled. "Tell her what you did."

"I placed an order based on the number of bed linens needed sixty years ago." He winced as he walked backward, talking to Corrie even as he followed Greer over to the dining room to get the table. "You know, back when the place had six guest cabins, each with two beds in them?"

"Ouch!" Corrie called back to him. "So where are all the extras?"

"Supply closet. Top of the stairs," Andy hollered above the sound of the table's metal stand scraping across the unfinished concrete floor.

Corrie took off and in a shot she returned with a sheet and a question. "So, I take it you also ordered way too many of those, um, golden-colored bedspreads, too?"

"Go ahead, say it." He peered at her from the side of the tree as he lifted it up onto the table.

"Say what?" She ducked beneath the branches to guide the base of the tree to the center of the heavy, dark wooden table.

"Whatever word you wanted to say before golden-colored? Ugly? Weird polyester? Guest repellant?"

Corrie laughed, backed out from under the newly

settled tree and stood upright to admire their handiwork. "Tacky."

Andy came to stand by her side, his attention aimed in the same direction as hers. "The tree?"

"The bedspreads," she clarified.

"Oh, yeah. Tacky or not, I have enough to last me through the next sixty years. So we're stuck with them."

"Unless..."

"They are nonreturnable," he muttered.

"I was just going to say, unless you tried something to jazz them up. What about letting the local ladies use them for quilt backing? Then you use some of their work on the beds and sell surplus quilts at the check-in counter."

"That's not a bad idea."

"Corrie never has bad ideas!" Greer grabbed Corrie around the middle and gave her a big hug. "I think we should keep her."

"Knock it off." Andy gave his sister a light tap on the shoulder. "She's not a lost puppy."

Strangely, Corrie felt exactly like a lost puppy. Only she felt that way when she thought of returning home, not here in the inn with Greer and Andy.

Andy went out and got the spare twinkle lights and began winding them through the branches.

Corrie showed Greer how to carefully poke a threaded sewing needle through the center of the popcorn and slide it along to the end. She left her with that and went to throw together some sugar cookie dough.

When she had popped the first batch into the oven she came back to find Andy with the lights tangled into a ball and Greer with only three pieces of popcorn strung, throwing fistfuls of the stuff at the branches and crying.

"I leave you two on your own for fifteen minutes and this is what happens?"

"Maybe we really do need you to stay," Andy teased then gave a sad smile and added, "Which means if I were you, I'd run for the hills while you still can."

Corrie gave him a shake of her head then went down on her knees by his sister. She scooped up the sock monkey left limp on the floor and offered it to Greer. "What's the matter, sweetie?"

The child took Buddy Mon-Kay in both hands and curled him into a tight hug. "This isn't working. The popcorn just breaks when I try to string it. I miss my mommy. If she was here, she'd know what to do to fix it."

Corrie lifted her gaze to Andy.

He let the knotted-up lights fall away and came to their side. He put his hand on Greer's back. "Hey, kiddo. You know Mom is off helping somebody else have a family of their own for Christmas. I got an email saying she'll be back on Tuesday. That's not too long for us to wait, knowing what good work Mom is doing, is it?"

The little girl looked up at him and sniffled. The tears in her dark eyes beaded on her black eyelashes, but once she swiped them away with the back of her hand, they stopped. "No. That's not too long. Families are important. I just wish…"

Andy's face went pale. His jaw tightened.

Clearly, even people who didn't have bitter, overprotective mothers sometimes wished their moms made different choices. A wall of conflicting emotions rose up in Corrie. She missed her mom. She wanted to comfort Greer. She had empathy for Andy. She felt in that one moment abandoned and comforted.

She stood and cleared her throat. "You know, I have three big bags of miniature marshmallows in the trunk of my car. I bet those would string a lot easier and be just as pretty. Why don't I go get those?"

Andy turned his head to follow her flight as she gathered her coat and headed for the door. "But they're for the contest entry, right?"

"Yeah. It's a quick way to make an easy fondant and I want to mix them with icing to make clumpy, shiny globs of snow. But they're just marshmallows. I can buy more tomorrow." With that she stepped outside and took a deep breath to collect herself.

What was happening to her? she wondered. Maybe Andy had a point about sticking to the plan. If she let herself get carried away too much, she'd never find her way. She took a deep breath, steadied her resolve and went to get the marshmallows from her car.

They did string up much more easily than the popcorn, especially after they decided to use dental floss instead of string. In almost no time they had wound the garland from the top branches to the lower ones. Andy plugged in the twinkle lights.

"Now we're getting somewhere," Corrie announced at the sight.

"Somewhere boring," Greer grumbled. "There's no colors on this tree. That doesn't look very Christmassy to me."

Corrie stared down at the very simply shaped, pale

sugar cookies on the tray in her hands. "She has a point. If I had food coloring, I could have whipped up some icing for these. But I didn't bring any because I wanted all white accents on my piece."

"You know these cookies are kind of like your contest gingerbread." Andy picked up one of the diamond shapes.

"How so?" Corrie cocked her head, trying to guess what he had in mind.

"They don't have to taste good." He looked over the cookie in his hand as if contemplating taking a bite. "In fact, they don't even have to be edible."

"I did make them extra thick and less sweet than my usual Christmas sugar cookies, to stand up to being hung on the tree. So, what are you thinking?"

He moved in close to whisper, "I have gallons of powder blue paint in the dining room. I don't suppose the painters would miss enough to cover a few cookies."

She pulled back just enough to meet his gaze. "Andy McFarland, I do believe you're beginning to think like me."

"I'd deny it but before I met you I can't imagine a case where I'd ever have suggested using wall paint on cookies, then using those cookies as Christmas tree ornaments." He shook his head and put the cookie back on the tray.

She laughed and went to the cans stacked along the side of the dining room. She picked one up and read the label. "You sure you ordered powder blue paint?"

"I don't like the sound of that question. What's wrong?" His boots scuffed over the concrete floor, pounding along until he was at her side. "What color is the paint?"

She plunked the can down with a deadened thud. "Gunpowder blue."

His eyes went all squinty. "What exactly is gunpowder blue?

Corrie used the can opener key to pry the lid off and peered down inside, concluding, "Gray."

"Gray?" He swept two fingers across the paint on the lid and smeared it on to the dining room wall.

Corrie looked closely at the color, which was darker and maybe a hint bluer than the concrete beneath their feet. "It's gray all right."

"No. This won't do. I can't..." His face went red.

Corrie suspected that if the painters had been here instead of her and Greer, he'd have lit into them and taken a bite out of their backsides. He had been trying so hard to get this all right and here it was, another goof up like the bed linens and lack of curtains and workers who refused to work in bad weather. She wanted to comfort him. She wanted to counsel him.

She wanted to take him in her arms and kiss him and make it all better, the way he had when she had bumped her head.

Instead she tried to smile about it and said, "At least you hadn't already wasted a couple of days getting it on the walls before you found out."

"Yeah, I guess there is that." He took the lid from her and set it on top of the can. "Well, there's no choice. I have tell the painters to hold off while I go to Daviston tomorrow to get all new paint."

Greer cocked her head and looked at them. "Does that mean we're done decorating?"

"We can find another way to get color on to the tree," Corrie said. There was always another way, of course, and Andy needed to be reminded of that. "If you have any colored paper we could make a paper chain."

Andy shook his head and nudged the paint can with the toe of his boot. "I don't know where I'd find any—"

"I have some." Greer ran off to the spot beside the front door where she had sloughed off her coat. Her small hand dove into the coat pocket and she wrestled free the piece of red paper she had brought home from Sunday school. "We can use this."

"That's a start. If you can round up some more, plus a pair of scissors and some glue or tape, we'll be in business." Corrie took the page.

"I have some tape in a box in my room and I have a magazine we could cut up, too. There's scissors in the kitchen drawer because Andy won't let me keep them upstairs." Greer ran off to get the other supplies.

"You know which drawer she means?" Corrie started off toward the other room with the paper in her hand.

Andy raised each can of paint in turn, checking the labels and shaking his head as he said, "Considering I was hiding them from her and she knows where they are, my guess is she moved them, so…"

"I'll figure it out as I—" Just then she flipped over the page Greer had gotten in Sunday School, wanting to look at it before she cut it up. With every sentence she read there, her stomach tightened. "Andy? Did you know that the kids have to come up with their own costumes for the Christmas pageant?"

"Huh?" He looked up from the paint cans at last and blinked as if he'd just woken up from a light nap. "What? Costumes? When?"

Corrie closed the distance between them, her boots scuffing lightly over the hard surface of the floor with each hurried step. She extended the paper to him. "They have to bring their own costumes to the dress rehearsal Tuesday evening."

"No. Not possible." He took the paper away from her, read it over. "A costume? With a *halo and wings?* Forty-eight hours from now when I have to go out of town tomorrow? It's not doable. No. There are some things I just can't…" He crumpled the paper into a ball in one hand. "I can't do it all."

"Hey! We need that for the paper chain," Greer snapped.

"I don't have time to fool around with paper chains or painted cookies or decorating Christmas trees." Andy tossed the balled-up paper lightly to his sister then paced to the base of the stairway, looked back at the unfinished room and shut his eyes. "I started out this day just a couple days behind on the inn. I've lost at least one more day because of the paint. Now I find out I'm also behind schedule getting you a costume for the Christmas play. I don't think I can do all this alone."

"You're not alone," Greer and Corrie spoke at once.

He put his fist on the banister and looked toward the door. "Look, it's not that I don't appreciate you two but neither one of you is a professional painter, neither one of you can make a child's costume out of, well, I don't even know what we'd make it out of but I do know we don't have a sewing machine to do it and if we did, either of you a seamstress?"

"I may not be any of those things but I'm a really good prayer." Greer took Corrie by the hand, dragged her a few steps then reached out to her brother. "You told me that we're never alone. God is always with us. That's what Christmas is all about, God loves us and doesn't want us to be alone, so He sent us Jesus. So when we think it's too much for us to take care of ourselves, we can turn to him."

Corrie and Andy looked at each other. Another defining moment, this time not just for Andy, but for all of them. What he did now would help to shore up the foundation of his sister's faith. And it would create a new level of closeness between Andy and Corrie. They would no longer just be two people whose paths crossed one lonely Christmas season. They would share a bond of faith.

"And one of the ways we help each other is to pray for each other," Greer went on. "If we do that then we know we aren't alone. We know Mom isn't alone when she's traveling and Andy's not alone when he's trying to get all his work done. And Corrie."

"What *about* me?" she asked softly.

"Even if you don't find your daddy, you're not alone. You have God. You have us."

Tears washed over Corrie's line of vision. She struggled to swallow. Hardly an hour ago she had felt like a lost puppy and had dug deep within her memory to hold fast to her mother's warning that she could only count on herself. Now this innocent child had taken her hand

and acted in God's stead to say that she was never alone because she was loved. Corrie looked at Andy.

"I have to tell you, if Greer wasn't here, I probably wouldn't have even thought about turning to prayer until I was absolutely overwhelmed."

She nodded.

"But…what do you say?" He held his hand out toward her.

Her hand trembled as she lifted it then stretched her arm out and slid her chilled fingers into the warmth of his palm.

There in the twinkling light of the Christmas tree she bowed her head and the three of them shared a brief prayer that everything would work out.

That night as she drove home, Corrie began to formulate her own idea of just how that would happen.

Chapter Twelve

Monday morning the alarm clock woke Andy. He went about his workday routine as always. Showering, dressing, then heading into Greer's room to get her up and started getting ready for school. Only this morning, Greer's bed was empty.

A week ago that would have either irritated or worried him, or both. Today, he headed downstairs fairly certain of where he would find his sister and who he would find her with.

"Good morning, Greer! Good morning, Corrie!" He strolled through the swinging kitchen door only to find the room dark and cold.

Confused, he headed to the dining room. Empty. His pulse picked up to match his footsteps pounding against the unforgiving concrete. He had his hand on the banister and was just about to go bounding upstairs to look for his sister when the sound of giggling made him pull up short. "What on earth are you two doing?"

"'Bout time you got up, sleeping beauty." Corrie called from where she sat, cross-legged on the floor shredding something silvery into strips that she then handed to Greer who reached up on tiptoe to place them on the tree. "We've already eaten breakfast out of a pouch and recycled the packaging into tinsel."

"Nothing you just said registered in my thick head." He rubbed his hand through his hair and squinted at the pair of them.

Greer laughed and handed him a silver packet containing a toaster pastry. "We ate them cold because I told Corrie that's how I like them and she said she'd rather eat the cardboard hot or cold and I said that if we have to take the marshmallows off the tree then we should at least make icicles out of—"

"Again. Head." He pointed to his skull. "Thick. Not getting any of this."

Corrie laughed and stood. "I went to the grocery store in Hadleyville last night after I left here and found out there wasn't a marshmallow to be found in all of town."

He blinked at her and decided that even if she insisted on not making any sense, that didn't mean he couldn't carry on like a civil, normal human being. "Good morning to you."

Corrie blushed.

He'd never met a woman so sheltered and yet so outgoing who blushed as easily as Corrie did. Well, he'd never met a woman as anything as Corrie. Still, he liked it when she blushed.

So he kept his gaze trained on her, folded his arms and lowered his chin. Using his best cool intensified look he asked, "I suppose you came to my home this early to get a start on your project?"

Her blush deepened. "Actually, no."

Greer began fiddling with marshmallow strings and moving around the tree. "She came to get a ride to Daviston with you."

Cool intensified became lukewarm unnerved. "What?"

"You said you were going over first thing to pick out some new paint?" Corrie made a nonspecific gesture toward the dining room and the pyramid of cans of gunpowder blue paint. "If you don't mind, I'd like to come with and see if I can't find some marshmallows."

"If she can't she may have to take the ones off the tree, only we've all had out dirty paws all over them." Greer held her hands up and flashed her fingers up and down. "So these marshmallows might not look very white and snowy. So she'd rather go with you. So…say you'll take her, Andy."

"I need to… I can't just…"

"And get some ornaments for the tree. Not a lot, but some pretty ones. Shiny. And lots of colors." Again, Greer waved her hands all around as she spoke.

Corrie stood perfectly still, her hands clasped in front of her looking like a hapless waif in search of marshmallows.

He shifted his gaze from Greer to Corrie then to the tree. "I'll be ready to leave as soon as Greer gets on the bus for school."

Greer cheered and leapt in the air.

That was way more enthusiasm than the situation merited. Corrie laughed at the kid's antics. But then she could. Corrie wouldn't have to deal with the aftermath when she left and Greer realized that neither her prayer nor her blatant matchmaking attempts would make Corrie his girlfriend.

He rubbed his hand over his forehead but that didn't ease the twinge of pain building there. He went to collect his sister to take her to the bus stop and though he didn't want to do it, he had to make it perfectly clear to the kid. "I'll take Corrie to Daviston because I'm going anyway, and it's a good thing to do what you can for others, that's all. Nothing more. Got that?"

"I got it," Greer had said as she skipped off. "But I'm still praying that Corrie is your girlfriend. Don't forget the ornaments."

This was not how he had expected the morning to go. Greer on the bus. Corrie in the seat next to him. The Snowy Eaves Inn in the rearview mirror. Still, it didn't seem to be costing him any time or effort and he didn't exactly mind the company.

"When we get to Daviston, we'll hit the home improvement store first to return the wrong color paint." He glanced back to the truck bed to indicate the cans that had been stacked in the doorway to the dining room since last night. And were still stacked in the doorway to the dining room at this very minute. He fixed his eyes on the road as they passed a sign saying they were only a few miles away from Daviston and he groaned. "No. I can't believe this."

Corrie didn't seem to have any trouble believing, or pointing out his mistake, though she did have the good grace to look sympathetic as she said, "You forgot the paint, didn't you?"

"I meant to put the paint in the truck but I got distracted." He gripped the steering wheel. "If we go back and get it now it will add at least an hour to this trip. And cost at least an hour of work today for me and... oh, man."

"You know, I took a lot of pictures of the inn and Christmas tree last night." She pulled her purse into her lap and began rummaging around in it. "I might have gotten the paint smudge you made on the wall if you want to show them how wrong it is. Worth a shot, right?"

She brought out her phone and began scrolling back through the photos.

Andy kept his eyes on the road. This was not like him. He didn't just up and leave to run an errand without making sure he had everything he needed. "Don't worry about it, Corrie. It's not just about the color. We left in such a rush I left the phone number of the painter's crew chief."

She set the phone in her lap, cocked her head and pushed up her glasses. "Okay. No problem. We'll just look him up on the web."

"Or, when we get to town we'll look him up in the phone book."

"The phone book?" She laughed like he'd suggested they do something as archaic as hopping in his jalopy and heading down to the burger joint to split a malted. "I've used a phone book maybe three times in my whole life. Why don't we just look him up online?"

He nodded toward the phone in her lap. "Can you connect to the web on that thing from here?"

She jabbed a couple of buttons. "Um...no. Sorry."

"Then when we get to town we'll try it the old-fashioned way. C'mon, you're the one big on being flexible when things don't go the way you want. Might do you good to learn a new skill," he teased. "It's not hard. The guy's name is Ben Haines. You go to the H's, find Haines then look down the list to Ben. Ben Haines… Haines, Ben."

"Haines, Ben. Haines… Ben." She said it normally, then quietly then she just mouthed the name with no sound at all. Then her lips moved without clearly forming any name or recognizable word. Finally, she turned to him. "What if…Andy…oh my goodness! It can't be that easy, can it?"

"Trust me, it is."

"No. You don't understand." She flipped back through the collection of photos she'd taken in the inn and stopped at one taken in the attic. She turned the screen toward him and thrust it in his direction. "BJ loves BB."

"I can't look at that. I'm driving. And if I weren't driving and could look at it, I would still have to tell you that I have no idea what you're talking about."

"My mom never talked about my dad to me. My grandmother insisted that Mom not even put his name on my birth certificate. I guess my mother went along with that because she was so hurt when he didn't come for her and she was alone and desperate and needed my grandmother's love and approval."

"I see." He made a sharp turn and the truck went bumping off the highway on to the side road that would take them to the store where they could use the phone book and get new paint.

Corrie seemed oblivious to the scenery as it changed from rural roadway to the landscape of a midsized town.

She just stared at her cell phone and said, "Ten years ago when I begged my mom to find my dad, she got on the phone immediately. I sat on the floor in the other room, listening as she asked again and again for James Wallace. James Wallace. I said the name over and over and wrote it down in my diary like that. But…"

"Your mom wasn't calling people and asking about your father, she was calling directory assistance, asking for a listing. Last name first."

"I know it sounds so obvious now, but I was a kid. I didn't know about that, I just heard her asking over and over for James Wallace but his name was really—"

"Wallace James."

"Wallace James," she echoed, softly. She touched the picture on the small screen. "Okay, that doesn't make the initials BJ. But in the same year my mom worked at the inn, someone with her initials loved someone with the last initial J. Andy, I think I just figured out my father's real name."

"I guess it would be a bad time to bring up that if you had approached this more carefully instead of making it up as you went along, you'd have had that information before you made a thousand-mile drive."

"I just…" Her lower lip quivered. "I feel so foolish. All that time, wasted. When if I had only…"

"I didn't say that to make you feel bad, Corrie. I was just trying to lighten the moment." And done a lousy job of it, judging from the stricken look on her sweet face. Fortunately, he had what he believed would be the perfect remedy for that. "I suspect you'll forgive me for that clumsy attempt at a joke when I tell you this. You know our mayor, Ellie Walker? The one with the nephew in Virginia named Wallace? Her maiden name was James."

"You mean I've been spending time all week looking for my dad right under the nose of my own..." She scrunched her face up like she was doing a tricky math problem in her head.

"Great aunt," he filled in for her as he pulled the truck into the parking lot and eased it into the closest available space. He shut the engine off and turned sideways in the cab to face her. "Ellie James Walker is your great aunt."

"Ellie *James* Walker is my great aunt." She bowed her head then sniffled.

He thought he should say something but had no idea what. He swallowed and felt like he had a baseball lodged in his chest. Ever since his dad died he had made it his goal to protect his family from every inevitability he could plan against. And to fix any damage left by whatever he couldn't plan around, whatever caught them off guard.

"What a silly mistake to make. Just blindly charging around with the wrong name when I should have... I could have..." A small sob cut her off. Her shoulders lifted and fell, then she covered her mouth with her hand and tried to collect herself.

Corrie was not his family, but when he brought her into his home and promised to set things right after Greer broke her treasured snow globe, he had extended that same dedication to her. And he had failed her. "Like you said, you got the wrong idea as a kid. You didn't know any better."

"What about my father? Did he not know any better?

If it could be that simple for me to find him, wouldn't it have been just as easy for him to find me? He knew my mom's real name and where she lived. She's owned a bakery in that town with her name on it for almost twenty years now." She shook her head slowly. "He could have found me, if he wanted me. My mom was right. We can only depend on ourselves."

Corrie Bennington sat in his truck crying over all the time lost, all the opportunities she might have taken that would have led her to her father so much sooner and the harsh reality that that father had never tried to make contact. Andy didn't know how to fix that.

She slipped her glasses off and tried to clean them with a corner of her green-and-white scarf. The spots from her tears and the fuzzy fabric created a cloudy blur that painted the entire lens.

Andy couldn't give her back the time lost or the sense of joy she had so clearly gotten from going about life in her haphazard, things-will-work-out-if-you-are-open-to-change way. But he could do this. He reached out and took her glasses, tugged free the hem of his fresh, clean shirt and carefully cleaned them. Then he reached out, tipped her chin up with one finger and slid the glasses in place.

He brushed his thumb over her cheek to wipe away a runaway tear and said, quietly, "When you know better, you do better. You have a name now. You have a connection. Corrie, you have what you came for. You went about it in a weird way, but you've reached your goal."

"Have I?" She looked up at him, attempted a weak smile then sighed. "Funny, from my point of view, it feels like I've lost sight of it completely."

Chapter Thirteen

Andy spent the next two hours tracking down the painters, dealing with their mistake, arguing with them when they said they couldn't come out to start his job until tomorrow and then looking at countless paint samples in almost imperceptibly differing shades of blue. Corrie sat on a stool in the paint store and stared at her phone. It was not her most productive morning.

Andy hated seeing her like this, this woman he'd seen chase after whatever she wanted—from a popover to a whole new life perspective—with joy and determination. He wished he understood her sudden bout of wishy-washiness. She had her goal within reach at last. She just needed to call her mother and confirm that she had the right name, just so she didn't bother some poor local family with her claim, then contact the mayor to find out how to reach her father. She just needed to get up her courage and follow through. Simple as that.

Simple as picking out a color for an inn you'd devoted every waking hour of the last year to completing. He winced, then glanced over at her and lifted up the two paint samples in his hands. "Blue or bluer?"

"The bluest." She slumped against the counter, her chin in her hand.

"The color for the dining room." He walked over to her and showed her the samples again, hoping to stir her out of her funk by giving her a chance to do what she seemed to love most—meddle in his business.

Her face did brighten up a bit. "You're going to let me choose the color for the dining room at the Snowy Eaves Inn?"

"Whoa. I didn't say I'd let you choose. It's still my baby, you know, but I would like your input." He meant that. She had good taste and a vested interest in the old inn.

"Can't let anyone else do a job that you had on your 'to-do' list, right?" She sort of smiled as she said it, but didn't give off the feeling she actually found any humor in her observation.

"Blue or bluer?" he asked again.

"My mom said I wasn't going to find what I was look-ing for in a museum or a photograph. I realize now, it's not even in a name." She rubbed the pad of her thumb lightly along the edge of her cell phone, frowned and looked off into space. "Maybe the truth is that I don't even know what I'm looking for, and until I do, I'm never going to find my way."

He'd only made the offer as a subtle way of helping her. But what had ever been subtle about Corrie Ben-nington? He tossed the paint samples down on to the counter, anchored himself directly in front of her and folded his arms. "Look, you want my opinion?"

She barely looked up from the phone. "I thought you wanted mine."

He took the phone from her and held it up like a lawyer offering a vital piece of evidence. "About that call you can't seem to make."

"Yeah, sure. Why not?" She snatched the phone away from him and sighed. "But I think I already know what you're going to say."

"Oh, you do, do you?"

"Same advice you've been giving me since I got here. Make a plan. Get things in their proper order, maybe even write up some notes for the conversation. Then just stay on track, don't let anything or anyone throw me off course."

"Actually, I—"

"And you know, you're right."

"I am?"

"Yes. You're right and I… I'm all wrong." She shook her head and met his gaze at last. "I've been going at this from all directions. Thinking every new avenue, every new person I met might just have something important to add. Hoping that if I kept my eyes, my ears, my heart, my options open I'd stumble on my answers eventually."

"That doesn't sound 'all wrong' to me, Corrie." In fact, the things she was beating herself up over were some of the very things he found most endearing in her.

"You're sweet to say it, but really, I can see now I've just been spinning my wheels. If I had listened to my mother to begin with, I'd have accepted that I have only myself to rely on. I'd have demanded she give me all the information I needed and probably found the man without all this gingerbread inn, wasting your time, decorating bandstands and cutting down Christmas trees nonsense."

"I never said you wasted my time." He wanted that made very clear.

"Well, then, let's not waste any more of it. Pick a color." She tapped the counter, missing the two samples Andy had selected and landing on a pamphlet of heritage colors with a blue wall on the cover. "We have ornaments, marshmallows and Christmas-pageant-costume supplies to get. That's what we came here for, that's the plan. Let's stick to it."

She marched off toward the door, leaving Andy to pick up the decorating pamphlet, peer closely at it then hand it to the man waiting to fill his paint-mixing order. "Four gallons of whatever color this is."

"It's all a matter of sorting things out and getting them done now. Shopping? Tick." She made a check mark in the air as she strode out the door. "Gingerbread contest entry? Tick. Phone calls to Mom, Ellie Walker, my father? Tick, tick, tick. No wild goose chases that lead nowhere. No more living in a fog like a kid who thinks that there's some wonderful place where she could go and find her answers. I had my answers, Andy. My mom and *you* were right all along."

The minute they got back into his truck, Corrie began to lay out a strategy. They'd go to a big discount store where they could get everything they needed in one place, return to pick up the cans of newly mixed paint and get back in Hadleyville in time for Andy to pick Greer up from school.

Andy couldn't have laid it all out better himself. That should have pleased him but seeing her like this, so focused on the goal and keeping one foot in front of the other to get to that goal kind of made him want to fog up her glasses and see if she wouldn't rather go try to find a civic club luncheon to crash.

"We can get this done faster if I gather the grocery items, you pick out the Christmas ornaments then we meet in the craft department to get what we need for Greer's costume." She breezed in and grabbed a shopping cart.

Andy had to hustle to catch up with her. "What? You're in too big a hurry to stop and make that poor elderly greeter your new bff? Or at least ask him if there's a lady's sewing circle meeting today that you can crash for the homemade pie?"

She gave him a sidelong look. "I don't have time for that now, Andy."

"Don't have time for pie or…jokes?" he asked quietly as she pushed purposefully on past him. She didn't answer.

His cell phone rang and she called out behind her without breaking stride, "Meet me in the craft section in ten minutes."

He watched her walk away and somehow even the way she carried off that pink coat and those chunky boots had changed. It was an act. He realized that. But still, an act born of pain and embarrassment. She could have found her father anytime, if she had been willing to accept her mother's bitter life view. Instead, she followed her own heart and where had it gotten her?

Here. It had gotten her here. It had gotten her to the Snowy Eaves Inn. It had gotten her to him. How could

Andy *not* be a bit sad to see her deny the part of her that did all that?

He cleared his throat and answered the phone as she disappeared from sight behind an oversized candy-cane-framed sign promising "Christmas savings on the things you need now."

Ten minutes later he strained to read the overhead signs searching for the craft section in the huge, brightly lit store. When he couldn't readily find it, he just began looking aisle by aisle through the bundled up shoppers for that familiar coat and boots.

"Nope. No. Uh-uh. Not…" He pulled up short, turned and went back two steps. Hands on hips he shook his head at what he saw. "Okay, I understand taking off your coat and tossing it in the cart, but where are your boots, young lady?"

"You like?" She stepped out into the aisle, placed one toe out and rolled her ankle.

Andy couldn't admire the bright white athletic shoe on her foot without taking in the view of Corrie head to toe. He'd grown too used to seeing her in her padded coat, shapeless boots, winter scarf, even that wrap-around bib apron that practically enveloped her when she worked in his kitchen. He hadn't realized how tiny she was, almost fragile, it seemed.

He'd never thought of her that way but looking at her with her boots and her coat in a cart looking like every other woman in the store…

"Why?" he asked.

She shrugged one shoulder to downplay it all and looked at the floor. "It's not going to snow while I'm here. It's time I accepted that. These shoes are practical. Don't you like them?"

He had liked her unfounded optimism. He had liked her being ready for her dreams to come true. The idea that she was now ready to kick all that to the curb, and wearing sensible shoes while she did it? He didn't like that one bit. He came to her and said softly, "I liked your boots."

She smiled up at him. "But these are for 'what is,' not for 'what if.'"

"But, Corrie…"

"You didn't get any ornaments?" She adjusted her glasses, giving him a stern look.

"I, uh, no…the call took longer than… It was the dispatcher at the company where we bought the reclaimed wood flooring."

"Problem?" She moved back behind the shopping cart and rolled it along, scrutinizing the shelves piled with glue and felt and beads and more.

"No. Actually, they plan to load our order up tomorrow and send it out Wednesday. We should have it by the weekend. We may have to point every fan in Hadleyville on to them to get the varnish to dry in time, but the floors should be installed and ready for guests by the open house on Christmas Eve."

"Great!" She paused to pick up two large jars of glitter. "Score another point for taking things on yourself and sticking with the program until you get results. Which do you think? Silver or diamond dust?"

"Honestly, Corrie, I think—"

"You're right. I said I'd do Greer's costume myself, that makes it my choice. I'll take them both." She clunked them into the basket. "So, I've got the new shoes, the replacement marshmallows and some candy canes and cinnamon sticks to put on the tree. Now all I need is some poster board and we can be on our way. What about you?"

He needed a great deal more than anything he could find in a superstore, he thought. In that instant, he recalled the prayer he had uttered the night Corrie showed up on his doorstep. He had asked the Lord for help.

Just a few days later, the final details for the inn had begun to fall into place. It actually looked like he might make the Christmas Eve deadline for the open house. On top of that, he'd shown Corrie how to fix her entry in the gingerbread house contest. And as of today, she not only knew her father's name, but had a lead on one of his—of her—relatives who could bring them together. Taking all that into account, it seemed like Andy had everything he needed and more.

He looked into the basket and then at Corrie. "Maybe we should get a few ornaments, just in case Mom doesn't get home tomorrow, for Greer."

"Okay, then." She gave a quick nod and wheeled the cart right by him. "We'll do that but you two are on your own to hang them up. I want to go back to my hotel room and do some research online with the new name I have for my dad. I don't expect anything new to turn up, but I should cover all the bases. If he really is the mayor's nephew, he doesn't even live in Vermont anymore, so I can backburner that until I've done what I came here to do, represent my mom's bakery in the gingerbread house contest."

"And see snow," he called out after her.

"I can't see it snowing, Andy. I just have to accept the way things are and keep my eyes on the prize."

"I thought the things you can't see with your eyes *were* the prize," he murmured as she walked away.

Chapter Fourteen

"Where's the sparkle? You promised sparkle." Greer's black dress shoes scuffed over the lobby's concrete floor as she twisted around to try to look at her cardboard-cutout wings.

"First things first, sweetie. I have to get them on and make sure they'll stay put and not droop." Corrie chewed on her lower lip.

Yesterday she might well have covered the wings in glitter as soon as she was happy with their shape and size and then worried about whether they worked for the costume. It would have been messier that way, and more fun. And it would have made Greer's eyes light up when she tried on the simple but adorable costume that Corrie had managed to whip up with another spare white sheet, some golden tinsel garland and poster board. But this way was better, she told herself. "Once we get the kinks worked out we can—"

Greer did another spin.

"Honey, you have to stand still."

"But I feel prettier when I twirl. Don't you think twirling is the best, Corrie?"

"We don't have time for twirling right now, no matter how pretty it makes you feel or what I think of it."

For the record, Corrie did think twirling was the best but clearly the things she thought were best didn't get her anywhere. Greer was right that all the sparkle had gone out of this whole costume bit, and Corrie didn't mean the glitter. She hung her head and sighed.

"Knock it off, kid. You're like a puppy chasing its tail." Andy came from the dining room into the lobby wiping paint off his hands with a rag. "Let Corrie do her job."

Corrie sat back on her heels. "That's as good as it's going to get for now. Go upstairs and take this off, sweetie, you can put it back on when we get to the church for the rehearsal."

"Oh, man, the rehearsal!" Andy scrunched his eyes shut tight and smacked his forehead with one open hand. "I forgot all about that. When do we need to leave?"

Greer and Corrie shared a look then both broke out giggling. Corrie pushed up from the floor, went to him and took the rag from his grasp. "We need to leave as soon as we get you cleaned up."

Greer scampered on upstairs.

"Aww, no." Andy raised his hand to the exact same spot where he'd left a streak of pale blue paint. "I didn't…"

"You did." She had to go up on tiptoe to reach his forehead, especially without the added oomph of her thick-soled boots. But if she rested one hand on his shoulder and stretched… "There. All better."

"I've said it before, Corrie, you do make everything around here better," he said quietly as he took the rag from her hand.

She lowered her feet to the floor. Another time, another circumstance, if she had stood this close to Andy and he had said that, Corrie doubted if her feet would touch the ground for days afterward. "Thanks."

"I only wish it were that easy to make it *all* better." He shut his eyes and his head shook slightly.

She studied his face for a moment. He had dark circles under his eyes and a grim set to his lips that he hadn't had when they had gone out to cut down the tree. "Problems?"

He leaned forward to put his mouth near her ear and whisper, "Got a text from Mom. Flights delayed. No details. Greer is going to be so disappointed."

"Oh, no." Corrie angled her shoulders back so she could meet his gaze. "What can I do to help?"

"You're doing it. Keeping Greer busy, making the costume. I can't tell you how much it means to me." He looked into her eyes.

Corrie pressed her lips together. Her head felt light and that lightness radiated through her arms and legs right down into her fingertips and toes. One more word from Andy…the right words…if he'd only ask her to stay. It wasn't part of the plan, of course. But if he would show the slightest inclination to change his plans…

"It means a lot to *us*," he corrected. "We'll never forget your kindness this week."

"Yeah." Corrie inched backward, her hand slipping from Andy's shoulder. Before her decision yesterday to not follow every whim, she might have pressed him for

more. Might have even told him outright that she was
open to helping out beyond this one week.

She took a deep breath as the conflict between the
things she had decided to be true and the things she had
always believed clashed within her. *You are on your
own. You can always find a friend to help you along
the way. Order brings results. You have to be flexible.
She would never see Andy McFarland again after this
weekend. She would see Andy everyday for the rest of
her life in her dreams of what might have been.*

"Ready to get going?" Greer bounded down the stairs
with her costume under her arm.

"Yes, it is time we moved on," Corrie said.

"I'll get my coat and my keys."

The rehearsal went smoothly. Well, as smoothly as
any rehearsal involving a dozen kids in costume on the
eve of a big chance to show off just one week before
Christmas could go.

Corrie had stayed to watch over Greer. She wanted
to see how the costume held up and get pointers on
possible additions or adaptations from seeing the rest of
the getups. And she did all that. She also avoided going
grocery shopping with Andy.

Grocery shopping seemed like such a mundane thing,
but walking through the store at his side, in the town
where he grew up, where her *father* had grown up? It
hinted at a sense of normalcy and belonging that weren't
Corrie's to claim. She didn't belong anywhere. She never
had.

That's what had brought her to the Snowy Eaves Inn.
That's what she had been looking for all along. That's
why she had chosen to spend time with the wonderful

people in Hadleyville rather than press them for info on her father. It was why she had stayed open to every possibility rather than lay out a set course and strive toward a practical goal. She had been hoping for something too wonderful.

She had been searching, not for a father or the right way to fit into her mom's work or even a snowfall to make her happy…she had been looking for a home.

It wasn't going to be Hadleyville, Vermont. Her father didn't live here. Her mother didn't live here. Andy wasn't going to ask her to stay here.

When the rehearsal ended and the children poured out of the church on to stone steps, Corrie tramped out in her plain no-name athletic shoes and splashed down in a big puddle of icy, mucky water. She grimaced and looked upward. "Rain?"

Greer squealed, pulled her coat up over her head and ran toward the street where Andy's truck sat. He flung open the passenger-side door for them.

Corrie sighed and started down the steps, muttering, "I thought for sure it would have snowed by now."

"Don't worry. Weatherman promises we'll be knee deep in the white stuff by Christmas," a woman said as she propelled her two children toward the curb.

"I'll be long gone by Christmas," she answered even though the family had already whisked past her.

She slouched in the seat next to Greer.

"Rehearsal that bad?" Andy asked, guiding the truck into the road.

She managed a laugh. "I'm a baker not a seamstress. The costume took longer than I expected and I still have to glitter the wings."

"And she's going to use lots of glitter," Greer insisted.

Corrie tried to calculate how long that would take, then leaned the side of her head against the cold glass of the window. "I just thought I'd have more done by this time today, what with doing things your way now."

"Yeah. Maybe I didn't mention that my way doesn't always mean a fast track." He chuckled and pointed the truck toward Mt. Piney. "But it's rocking and rolling now so how about you work on your contest entry while I make us all dinner?"

Forty-five minutes later Corrie had put the costume away, assured Greer that she'd decorate the wings before she left tonight then settled into the kitchen at long last. She had begun the process of making fondant when Greer came bounding in with her sock monkey wrapped in a bit of scrap sheet and a pair of cardboard wings taped to its back.

She set the toy aside and climbed on a stool next to Corrie. "What's that for?"

Corrie worked over the soft, pliant fondant and explained what she intended to do with it and that they'd have to let it rest before shaping it into snowdrifts and so on. "The real thing that has me worried is that before I can do anything else, I have to cover the entire roof with these little chocolate wafer candies. I brought as many as I could from home hoping I'd find some more here, but since I didn't, I can't afford to make even one itty-bitty mistake."

That from the queen of mistakes of all sizes. Her penchant for flying by the seat of her pants had come around to bite her yet again. She took out her frustration kneading the fondant. She was in such a rotten mood today. Maybe she should just chuck it all for tonight, go back to her hotel and work extra hard tomorrow.

"Painters finished the primer coat. Once they've gotten all the work around the trim, they're going to call it a day." Andy came in and went straight to the sink to wash his hands. "So that leaves me free to get dinner on the table."

"Corrie is going to use chocolate candy for the roof of her inn, Andy," Greer reported.

"Hey, that's a cool idea. If we ever get a leak in our roof, I'll remember that." He dried his hands on a kitchen towel then motioned for his sister. "Why don't you come over here, Greer, where you can hand me the ingredients for the casserole."

"Where I can't reach the gingerbread house and mess it up is more like it," Greer grumbled, wriggling down off the stool and going to Andy's side. "Man, you drop one snow globe and nobody trusts you, never again."

"We trust you, short stuff, just not with things that can't be easily fixed that have to be done by a certain time." Andy handed the girl two cans of condensed soup and pointed her toward the can opener. "I trust you with our dinner, if that's any consolation."

She rolled her eyes and promptly dropped a can of soup on his foot.

He let out a yelp and hopped around for a second before he gave Corrie a grin and a wink much to Greer's delight.

"Construction boots. Steel toes." He bent down and handed the dented can to Greer. "Now you see why you're on casserole duty and not going near that gingerbread house."

Corrie started to tell him that she didn't mind if Greer worked on the piece. Before she could, the whirr of the can opener cut her off.

Andy put one hand on the counter to create an intimate zone between them, lowered his head and said, "I want you to know I haven't forgotten about your snow globe. I said I'd figure out a way to make it right and I will."

The things Corrie wanted set right, Andy couldn't fix. He couldn't make up for all the conflicts stirring around in her about her father. He couldn't, and *wouldn't,* even if he could, tell her that her mother was wrong and Corrie should rely on faith and hope and friendship along with her own wits to get by. But when she looked up at his kind, handsome face?

She wanted to believe him. She wanted to allow herself to rely on him, to trust without cynicism. She mustered a fragile smile and met his gaze, so close that she could see the reddish tint to the tips of his eyelashes. "You don't have to worry about it, really."

The can opener went silent.

"I'm not worried." He stood up straight and folded his arms. "I'll get it done."

Corrie pressed her lips together and nodded. If she had tried to speak she'd have lost her voice and probably found herself blinking away the tears. She wanted her world to be the way it was the day she first arrived here. She wanted...

"Soup's ready," Greer called out over the bang and

clatter of cabinet doors opening and shutting. "What can I open next? Sardines? Coffee? Baked beans?"

"Better take care of this." He gave her a nod then turned to deal with Greer.

Corrie hunkered down over her project and began carefully laying out the chocolate wafers so as not to waste a one.

When Andy and Greer finished assembling the casserole, he went to the school backpack in the corner of the kitchen and handed it to her, knowing she had a reading assignment that she could just finish before dinner was ready. As the child got down to that he came over to inspect Corrie's progress.

"Nice work." He moved close in behind her then around to the side. "You see any room for real-world application with this method?"

"Is that renovation contractor speak for 'can you do some work around this place'?" She dipped her finger in a glass of lukewarm water and smoothed down a bead of icing before delicately pressing another wafer in place.

"No." He dipped his own finger into the icing bowl and then took a taste. "That is guy-standing-around-with-nothing-to-do speak for 'maybe this would go faster if you had a guy who has actually been on the roof of the Snowy Eaves Inn sticking those wafer things on on the other side'."

She looked up at him and smiled. "Very precise work to get the layers just like this. Think you can handle it?"

He adjusted his sleeves, which were already pushed up from cooking, then waggled his fingers like a street performer preparing to carry out an intricate sleight of hand. "Watch and learn."

Andy worked steadily away on one side of the roof while Corrie worked on the other. They didn't speak much. She could have chalked that up to concentration or even the weariness of the day or her anxious mood. But in truth, every time she raised her head to share a thought or witty remark or launch into a story about baking or Greer or what she hoped to do about the whole father-finding situation, she'd look at him working away and end up sighing. Just sighing.

What a nice guy. Strong guy. Take-charge guy. Why did he have to live a thousand miles away? It didn't seem fair. She wondered if those very thoughts had gone through her mother's mind all those years ago when she met Wallace James.

Now that she had a real name and a new perspective on what it meant to search for someone, how little effort it would have taken on his part to find them, Corrie saw her mother in a new light. How hopeful she must have been. And in love. So in love she had convinced herself that the two of them could overcome all the odds stacked against them. So that, when it all fell apart, it wasn't just her heart that was broken, it was her trust in the way she believed her life would play out.

Corrie had had a little taste of that today. Despite her mother's fear of being hurt, and her determination to teach Corrie to protect herself, Corrie had always taken chances. She'd always trusted God, the basic goodness of most people and her own common sense. Was that so wrong?

She looked up from her work to find Andy staring at her. She smiled, just a little.

He grinned at her. "Hungry?"

She hesitated. Not because she wasn't sure if she was hungry but because once again she didn't know if she could put herself in a situation with Andy and his sister that would only remind her later how very much alone she really was. The Corrie who had first shown up here days ago wouldn't have even considered that. She'd have done what felt right, expected the best outcome and if she ended up lonely and missing the good times, she'd have consoled herself that at least she had *had* those good times and celebrated that. She raised her head and looking at the man, thinking of his promise to make things right and the effort he had made already, a sliver of the old feelings peeked through.

Corrie smiled back. "I am hungry. Thank you for sharing your dinner with me."

A few minutes later they had heaping plates in the cozy kitchen. To keep Greer away from the paint fumes, Andy had vetoed eating in the dining room. Greer pointed out that it also kept her away from the big sawhorse tables weighed down with the opened paint cans with the lids tapped back into place. And the trim work balanced across the backs of tarp-draped chairs to make them easier to paint. Not to mention the wrong color paint stacked like cans in a carnival ready to be knocked over.

Andy held up his hand to stop her from adding to the list and laughed at being caught once again manipulating his kid sister's environment to make things easier on himself. The guy had a sense of humor about himself.

And he could cook, too.

Corrie filled up on the delicious casserole. The three of them laughed and talked about the pageant practice. Greer went into elaborate detail about how she wanted her wings glittered and never once mentioned her mother's delay. Andy listened intently and decided that he could wait until they were done to check on the job the painters had done.

When the McFarlands gathered the plates to rinse and put in the dishwasher, Corrie returned to work. More relaxed than she had been earlier, it only took a few minutes before she had tweaked the last few wafers into place on her side of the roof.

"There. Perfect." She stepped back and held her hands up. "Exactly the way I envisioned it. How's your side coming along?"

Andy and Greer both turned at the same time. Andy opened his mouth but Greer got her opinion out first. "Lousy."

"Hey!" Andy scowled at his little sister. "Why don't you go get those wings so we can finish up with those?"

"Very funny, you two." Corrie came around the island where they had been working fully expecting to find the roof as a mirror image or better of hers. She rounded the structure, and turned her head from the faces of her friends to the neat rows of chocolate wafers.

Only neat was not the right word for what she saw.

"Oh. Um, that's kind of…" She spread her fingers and jabbed them together so that they didn't quite fit. "Just in that one place, though. The rest of it is good. I mean…if you don't look too close at—-"

"He busted every wafer on that whole section by the pointy part," Greer volunteered, tipping up her chin and tossing her black hair in a smug sort of flip before heading out the swinging door. "And he wanted to keep *me* away from it."

"Sorry." He rubbed the back of his neck. "Blame my big, clumsy, calloused hands."

"I don't think they're clumsy." Corrie liked his hands. They were rugged enough for his line of work and gentle enough to braid Greer's hair. How could you not like hands like those? "This just isn't your forte."

"I was thinking I'd chip off the broken ones and the ones that slid a little then replace them with—"

"I don't have enough wafers to do that." She brushed her fingertips over the imperfections in Andy's handiwork. The broken bits and wobbly row made her smile. A real smile. A smile that came from the depths of her being. Life wasn't perfect, no matter how hard you tried, no matter how much you planned or followed the rules or stayed on schedule. That wasn't the end of the world.

"Oh, Corrie, I'm sorry, I—"

"It's no big deal." She looked up at him. All day she had tried her best to be a stick-to-the-schedule, stay-on-track kind of person. Now, Andy's little mess up gave her a reason to chuck all that and go back to improvising and making do with what God gave you. "I'm going to use a gloppy white frosting-type stuff to represent snow. I'll just make sure to glop a little extra over your bloopers."

"Corrie Bennington, you are the first woman I have ever met who offered to glop over my bloopers."

Okay, she blushed. *Again.* And laughed. She had blushed and laughed more in the last few days than she had this whole past year, she believed. She liked it. She lowered her face, then looked up at the man responsible. "You know what I mean. I just cover up the irregularities with a little snow."

"Snow!" Greer came bursting through the swinging door but instead of coming all the way in she stood there, holding it open.

"Not real snow," Corrie told the child. "Frosting made to look like snow. We can use it to hide your brother's roof goofs. Couldn't exactly use real snow for that, huh?"

"Well, if you wanted to, all you'd have to do is go outside and scoop some up!"

"What?" Corrie looked at Greer, then Andy. "Really? A real snow?"

"Big, fat, fluffy flakes." Greer swooped her hands down gracefully to demonstrate how they were falling. "It must have started a while ago because it's sticking already."

Corrie could hardly catch her breath. She stared at the gingerbread inn, the copy of the snow globe that she had so often dreamed of seeing blanketed in a real, honest-to-goodness snowfall. What had started as a real stinker of a day had totally turned around. Not by Andy's plans or Corrie's determination, but by a wonderful surprise.

"C'mon." Corrie looked up to see Andy holding her coat out to her. "You may get to use those boots after all."

Corrie didn't care about coats or boots or scarves or anything. She dashed past the man without stopping.

He snagged her arm and began tucking her into her coat.

"Hurry up. I want to see the snow," she protested.

"You're like a kid," he told her as he had to bend at the knees to see to get the coat fastened up right.

Greer clapped her hands. "Can I put on my coat and go out, too, Andy?"

"Sure. Wear a hat and gloves," he reminded her as he popped the collar of Corrie's coat up around her ears and brushed the hair back from the temples of her glasses. "I don't suppose you have a hat and gloves?"

"I'll be fine." She had already begun to jostle up and down trying to get him to turn loose of her so she could get going.

"I'll get you a pair of mine." He looped her polka-dot muffler around her neck, pulled it up like a hood on to her head then wound it around. "You can wrap up in this scarf to keep your head and face warm. Just as long as you don't stay out too—"

"Stay out? I can't even *get* out." She gave him a playful push then used the moment to spin around and make her getaway.

Andy was right behind her.

Corrie had actually seen snow falling a time or two in her life. Once, they'd even had a dusting of the white stuff on the lawn. It had practically shut down the entire town for a day. The grocery stores were depleted of bread and milk. Her mom did a record business in hot chocolate and cookies.

But nothing about those experiences had readied her for what she saw when she went skating out the door of the Snowy Eaves Inn.

"It's like a Christmas scene from a wonderful old movie," she said to Andy as he rushed out after her, wearing one pair of gloves and holding another set in one hand.

"Here, put these on."

"Oh, stop it." She pushed his hands away. "I don't want to put those on. I want to feel this. I want to feel the snow on my face and touch it with my bare fingers."

She moved out from under the shelter of the entryway and raised her face skyward. Bits of crystallized cold dropped on to her cheeks and instantly began to melt. The wind stirred and the flakes plastered themselves on her glasses and clung to her lashes.

"You're going to freeze," Andy warned her.

"I don't care if I do," she said and did a slow spin, arms wide and eyes shut. "Tell Greer she's wrong. Twirling is not the best. Twirling in *snow* is the best."

"All right, enough." He caught her by the hand and let her finish her whirl right into his arms. "Let's get these gloves on you and then—"

"We can make a snowman?"

"Not nearly enough snow yet. Besides, with all that rain we had this afternoon, there'll be a layer of ice out there. You need to be extra careful moving around, especially without your boots."

"Oh, you, with your boots and gloves and hats." She rested her hands on his thick coat and tipped her head back to look at his face. "What are you worried about?"

"You," he said softly.

"You don't have to worry about me," she murmured in return. She meant that.

"I don't? Why not? Because you're going to look after yourself?"

"Maybe. Or maybe because I'm going to look out for you." She hadn't planned it. Of course not. She didn't plan much of anything in her life. She couldn't be like Andy. Or like her mother. She followed her heart and believed in the best.

That's exactly what she did when she threw her arms around Andy McFarland's neck and standing in her very first, honest-to-goodness snowfall kissed him like she had never kissed anyone in her entire lifetime.

And like so often was the case when she didn't think things through, she regretted it almost instantly.

Chapter Fifteen

His strong arms folded around her, making her feel small and safe and as if no one else in the world existed. Her legs went weak. Her fingers, which had begun to stiffen with the cold, tingled down to the very tips. She was in Andy's arms. For the first time in her life, she felt she was where she truly belonged.

"Wow! It happened! It happened! Andy got a girlfriend for Christmas!" Greer peered out the door but didn't come outside.

"No." Andy took Corrie by the shoulders and put some space between them. "Corrie is *not* my girlfriend. This is not the answer to a prayer."

Where once there had been the two of them in each other's arms and a kiss that fanned the flames of the emotions that had been building in them all week, now a cold wind whipped between her and Andy.

Corrie brushed the back of her bare hand over her still trembling lips and shut her eyes. Andy had not meant to hurt her with his reaction. He'd been caught off guard. He hated getting caught off guard and had little patience with having to come up with new directions on the fly. So she'd help him out a little.

She placed her hand lightly on the man's arm and bent to speak to his excited little sister. "What Andy means, Greer, honey, is—"

"I said what I meant."

"Oh." Her palm dragged over the suede of his coat as she dropped her hand from his sleeve.

"I wanted to tell you I can't find my boots. Can I come out without them?" Greer said softly, her precious little face crestfallen. "But now I don't want to."

"Greer!" he called out after her.

The door shut.

He hung his head and flexed his gloved fingers. He shifted his boots to backtrack physically as he shut his eyes tight and muttered, "I'm sorry, Corrie. That came out harsher than I intended, but I have charge of Greer's physical, emotional and spiritual well-being here. Without Mom here, it's all up to me."

"Of course, the great Andy McFarland couldn't possibly need any *help*. He can do everything all by himself." That also came out harsher than *she* intended. It's just that her rotten day had finally seemed to turn around and now…

Now she just wanted to get out of here and deal with all this tomorrow.

"I'm sorry. This has all gotten way off track." She took another step away. Her foot slipped. The treads of her inexpensive shoes couldn't create enough traction to grip the snow and ice-covered sidewalk. Her breath snagged in the back of her throat as her stomach lurched and she pitched backward.

Andy lurched out to snag her by the arm but she shooed him away, grabbing on to the column that supported the portico instead.

"Look, I'm just trying to make sure that Greer doesn't come away from her stay with me thinking that prayer is like some online shopping site. Place your order and expect delivery in two to seven days."

"And that's admirable. But did it ever occur to you that by snapping at her like that you might send the message that you don't think God ever answers prayers?" She clutched the column and worked to get her feet under her. "Have you even tried to point out that what she's seeing might not be an answer to her prayer but to mine?"

He cocked his head and rubbed his thumb over the bridge of his nose. "Yours?"

"I prayed to see snow." She took a small step of faith, turned loose of the inn and held her hands out to her sides. "And here it is. I'm sorry if I let my excitement get out of hand about that."

"You have nothing to apologize for." He lowered his thumb to touch his lower lip then smiled and held that hand out to her. "I'm fine with it."

"I know you think that's a good answer, Andy. As long as you're fine and in charge and things are going your way…" She threw her hands up and groaned. "Speaking of going, I need to get moving before the roads get bad."

"They're already bad enough, Corrie, especially for someone who doesn't know how to drive in snow on top of ice." He kept his hand extended toward her. "Give me a minute to get my keys and I'll drive you back to the Maple Leaf."

"I don't need you to do anything else for me, Andy." She stuck her hand in her pocket and pulled out her own keys. "I'll be fine. I'll come back tomorrow, finish the inn and get it out of your kitchen."

"Corrie, you can't—"

She turned and marched toward her car, slipping at least twice along the way but managing to right herself.

He sighed loudly enough to make himself heard even as she walked away, then called, "I'll go inside and get your purse."

"My purse." Corrie flinched. She'd need that, of course, for her license and room key and money. Not only did that oversight make her fabulous exit scene fall flat, it reinforced Andy's notion that her capricious approach to life was really half-baked. She clenched her teeth and turned to say— "Who-oo-a!"

Her feet went flying out from under her. She flashed like a fish out of water, wrenching her body around, her arms flailing, and latched on to the fender of her small hybrid car.

"Stay put. I'll get my keys and we'll take you back over to Hadleyville."

"You can't tell me what to do," she called back. With one shove and a lot of false bravado, she righted herself enough to get to her car door and tug it open. "I'm going to warm up the car then drive up to the door. You can just leave my purse out front."

"I'm not going to leave your purse, or *you,* out here.

You're not going anywhere without me. I'm taking you and that's the last of it." He went inside.

Corrie plopped into the seat. She slammed her car door and jabbed the key into the ignition.

The engine seemed to side with Andy's assessment that she wasn't going anywhere without him.

"C'mon. I can't stay here or depend on that man after I kissed him like that, then told him off." She didn't believe the engine actually heard her, but after a few more tries, it growled. It sputtered. Finally, it sparked and started. "Okay. I can do this."

She put the car in gear and pressed her foot lightly on the gas. The car began to roll. She gripped the wheel. She *could* do this. Just move slowly, exert a steady but firm pressure to guide the car.

The wheels turned. The car moved, only not in the direction she had been guiding it. Slamming on the brakes did not fix that. The small car went skidding in what she imagined must have been a graceful spiral through the parking lot.

Corrie's performance was less than graceful. She stomped on the brake. She yelled at the top of her lungs for the car to stop. She looked to the still-closed door of the inn willing Andy to appear. If he did, she didn't know because seconds later she couldn't see the building anymore.

Once, twice, three loops then back end first off the lot and into the shallow ditch she went. Her heart pounded. She could hardly breathe. She made a quick mental survey. No pains. No injury but to her pride. She laid her head on the steering wheel.

A sharp rapping on the window startled her into look-ing up and finding Andy and Greer peering in at her.

"The Chinese judge gives you a..." Andy looked down at Greer.

She held up all of her fingers, spread wide. "Ten!"

Corrie could have just cried. She could have crawled down deep into her car and told them to leave her there to freeze and put them all out of their misery. Instead, she laughed. It was the ultimate example of rolling with the punches. As Andy assisted her out of the car, she looked him right in the face and said, "I've decided not to drive myself home tonight."

"Yeah! Corrie is staying!" Greer took the purse from Andy's hand and headed for the door of the inn. "Us girls can have a slumber party in the lobby by the Christ-mas tree and watch it snow all night long."

"I'll still take you to the Maple Leaf if you want," Andy said as he slung her car door shut and followed her making her way back to the parking lot. "But you're welcome to spend the night here. You know, like Greer said, you and she having a slumber party. Me tucked safely away upstairs."

"You mean you'd trust me, after that wild kiss I gave you?" Making light of the situation had worked a minute ago, Corrie decided to try it again. And if she got to hear Andy ask her to stay, even for just this one night, or tell her that he trusted her, even in good-natured jest, well, that wouldn't be so bad, either.

"I have Greer as a chaperone. She's so watchful in fear of something getting into the inn, she won't let you get out of her sight all night."

Another really crummy answer, she thought. But a

truthful one. She smiled and gave a half shrug. "Okay. At least if I'm out here I can keep working on my contest entry until the roads are cleared."

But the only reason she went into the kitchen again that night was to make a snack that Greer had insisted they needed. Only by the time she brought the tray with hot chocolate—heavy on the milk, light on the chocolate to help with sleep—and cookies out, the eight year old had drifted off.

Corrie settled the tray down on the floor between the two mattresses Andy had brought down for them to cushion against the hard concrete. She arranged the triple thickness of golden bedspreads, layered on for warmth, to cover the child then bent to give her a kiss on the head.

"Thank you."

It should have startled her to hear Andy's hushed voice in the large room lit only by the twinkling lights of the Christmas tree. But it didn't.

She looked up from where she knelt on the floor. "Thank *me?*"

"It occurred to me that you've thanked me several times. For my opinions. My expertise. My tallness. My kitchen. My ability to find my way around my own church." He came to her and offered a hand up.

She slipped her fingers into his and stood before him with Greer at their feet, the tree and the two-story windows to one side.

"You even thanked me for things I have no control over, like this snow." He turned his head toward the scene outside. The flakes whirled in the wind like millions of bits of down falling, dancing against the near-black sky. It had begun to collect on the limbs of the tall pines and blanket the ground to reduce the rocks and bushes to bumps and suggestions of shapes. "I just thought it was time I made it clear that it's me who should be thanking you."

She cast her eyes down and for once she didn't blush. She didn't feel ill at ease or embarrassed by her own misplaced or reckless feelings. He hadn't said any of the things she had so wanted him to say and yet, she had such peace about his nearness and her own place in his world, even if that place was only temporary. "I haven't done anything."

"You've done plenty and you know it," he whispered. "And now that it looks like the inn is going to get finished on schedule and you're going to find your father, maybe we'll both have some time soon to—"

He moved in close.

She tipped her head up.

He put his arms around her.

She drew in a breath, thinking she should say something. But no words could express what she felt to be here by the Christmas tree in the Snowy Eaves Inn with a real snowfall outside with Andy.

He kissed her softly on the lips, then on the cheek then finally on the forehead. "We'd better say good night now."

She nodded, still unable to speak.

"Sweet dreams," he said as he backed away.

"I plan on it," she said softly. Though she couldn't imagine any dream as sweet as this evening's reality. Tomorrow, everything would look different, she knew. The snow, the condition of her car, even the dining room when the painters got the new blue color on the wall. She had no idea how she and Andy would view their relationship by the light of day and the harshness of her realities. But for this night, Corrie could have peace and love and—

"Did you hear that?" Lying low on her own mattress, with the bedspreads thrown over her head and clasped tight under her chin, Greer's expression seemed even more anxious than her hurried whisper sounded.

"Greer, I didn't hear anything." Corrie lifted her head slightly to look out the window. "But if you did, it was probably just an animal moving around in the snow."

"Yeah, a bear moving around in the snow looking for something to eat, and when it can't find anything it could come in here."

Corrie yawned. "Bears hibernate in the winter."

"Great. If it's not a bear then it's probably a bad guy."

"Why would a bad guy come all the way out here in a snowstorm?" Corrie shifted her weight to try to get more comfortable on the thin mattress so she could get a little bit of sleep and have a shot at those dreams before daylight reordered her world. "It's nothing. Go back to—"

A muffled clunk cut Corrie off midsentence.

"You heard it, too, that time, didn't you?"

A crunching noise followed, then a low guttural sound.

"We should yell for Andy," Greer whispered, then took a deep breath.

"No!" They had said good night on such a perfect note of mutual appreciation. It could well be the basis for a whole new way of looking at each other. Corrie couldn't bear the thought of him rushing in to rescue her from something she could easily have avoided with a little forethought—*again*. "Don't yell! I can—"

Corrie lunged across to the other mattress. The mugs of once hot chocolate crashed against the hard floor.

Greer yelped once quietly then louder when the front door of the inn went banging open and a darkened figure stood framed against the hushed background of the snowy night.

"Get in the kitchen," Corrie commanded Greer in a raspy whisper. "It's probably a lost traveler like I was, looking for shelter from the storm but just in case... Andy left his ax by the tree over there. I'm going to get that."

"Should I—"

"Go!" The concrete stung against Corrie's bare feet as she stumbled and staggered over to the wall where Andy had leaned the ax yesterday. Her fingers found the handle and gripped it but she wasn't strong enough to raise it more than a few inches off the ground.

The intruder seemed completely unaware of her in the inky corners of the room. It crossed the threshold, stomping snow from its boots.

A thief or someone with evil intent wouldn't care whether they tracked snow inside, would they?

Their unexpected guest pushed the door shut, quietly.

Sneaky, Corrie thought. Whoever this is doesn't want to wake anyone. A traveler would be calling out to alert people, to ask for assistance. Her stomach knotted. She wished Andy were here to help but since he wasn't, she'd have to improvise.

"Stay right there and tell me who you are."

The figure raised its arms but said nothing.

Gathering all her strength, Corrie dragged the ax a few steps and tried again to lift it.

Just then the figure found the light switch, flipped it, yanked back the hood on her coat and the knit scarf from her face to reveal the red-headed woman Corrie had seen in the photo in Andy's office and said, "I'm Hannah McFarland. Who are you?"

"I'm…" Corrie released her grasp on the ax handle. The heavy-bladed tool went skidding and spinning over the smooth concrete floor, right toward the sawhorse holding the paint cans.

"Oh, no!" Corrie ran after it but couldn't get there in time.

The handle took out one set of table legs, causing the can of paint on that side to fall, roll and knock over the pyramid of cans of gray paint. The top one toppled and globbed its contents all over the floor and lower part of the wall. If Corrie had spent hours calculating all the angles, placing every stage just so and set it all up to cause a fantastic cascade of catastrophe, it could not have wreaked more havoc.

The sudden drop of one side of the sawhorse created a catapult effect, flinging a second can of paint, this one the new light blue color, on to the wall…and the floor… and ceiling…and windows…and a little bit on Andy's mom.

"Andy is going to blow up when he sees what I've done."

"I had a hand in this mess… Corrie? *You're Corrie,* aren't you?" She held out her hand.

"You know my name?" Corrie slid her own hand into the other woman's, gave it a shake then pulled it away, paint smearing her palm and fingernails. She looked around for a place to clean it off. "How do you know my name?"

"Andy mentioned you in his emails."

"He…he did?" Corrie's breath snagged in her chest.

"Greer told me all about you on the phone. Neither one of them mentioned you staying here, though."

"Oh. I…I'm stuck because of the snow. Andy's upstairs with his door shut. He said something about keeping the radio on so he couldn't hear us downstairs. Greer and I are having a slumber party." She motioned toward the mattresses on the floor then toward the kitchen door. "She's in the kitchen now."

"Wonderful! I can't wait to see my girl." Andy's mother wiped her hand on the wall.

Corrie gasped. "Shouldn't we clean this all up?"

The woman took a long, sweeping gaze then sighed and shook her head. "I am too bushed to bother with this tonight. It's only paint. Andy won't be happy but it's fixable. He's a fixer, my Andy."

"But all his plans—" Corrie's stomach knotted. This would throw a real monkey wrench into Andy's schedule and it was all her fault.

Mrs. McFarland didn't seem the least bit concerned, though, as she headed off to see her daughter.

This whole trip had just been one disaster after

another. Or, if you looked at it another way, one learning opportunity after another. Why should tonight be any different? She sighed and left her own handprint on the wall then followed after Andy's mother, thinking she'd figure out what to do about all this in the morning.

Chapter Sixteen

Andy slept until almost nine that morning. He'd slept with the door shut for propriety's sake, and because he thought Greer might wake up and start giggling and keep him awake, he'd left the radio on to an all-night talk station. Since no one had bothered to wake him and when he listened at the top of the stairs he heard only silence, he worried that the girls had overslept as well.

He came downstairs, on high alert, not wanting to startle anyone, but definitely concerned. A *whomp* and a *splat* made him practically jump out of his sweat-pants. A big, lightly packed snowball exploded against the lobby window.

Greer's laughter reached his ears first. Then Corrie's. He hurried on down the stairs toward the sound, trying to decide between making a face at the windows for the girls to use as target practice and going to the front door, scooping up a mound of snow and throwing it at the first person brave enough to try to get back inside.

His bare feet slapped down on the icy concrete and that made up his mind for him. "Face," he muttered, rubbing his eyes. "Definitely face. If the floor is this cold inside, I don't even want to know how bad—"

If he had been the kind to curse, he'd have let out a doozy just then. Instead he stood, transfixed. Frozen. Sucker-punched by the sight that welcomed him when he rounded the end of the stairs and looked into the dining room.

"Hey, sleepyhead, we thought we'd let you catch up on your beauty sleep so you'd be rested before you saw what went on here last night." Corrie came hustling into the lobby and began taking off the pair of gloves he had loaned her by tugging at the fingertips with her teeth.

"Uh, I don't suppose you could—"

"Andy! We got a snow day!" Greer chose to stomp the snow off her boots all across the lobby floor rather than slip out of them by the door as she should have.

"Why are you—"

"Good morning, sunshine!" Out of seemingly nowhere, his mom came in, bringing up the rear.

"Mom? When did you get here? I thought your flight was delayed." He rubbed his eyes again then jerked his thumb to the disastrous mix of paint and broken equipment and trimwork littering the dining room. "You don't happen to know anything about this."

"I know it was an accident and in the end, it's just a little paint and a few splinters. That's why we decided not to wake you last night about it." His mom came up and kissed him on the cheek, then dealt with the smear left by her lip balm by licking her thumb and rubbing it off his face.

"Stop it." He jerked away then looked at the three of them staring at him as if he were acting badly. Corrie had known about this and kept it from him? Greer didn't seem to even care how she treated his inn? His mom had flown all the way from China to mock his work? "Stop it, all of you. Doesn't anyone here have any respect for my property? My face? My feelings?"

They all stopped.

"What has you in such a sour mood this morning?" His mother began unwinding the muffler from around her neck.

"Oh, I don't know. Call me cranky but having all my hard work to finish my inn before I lose it forever destroyed while I slept will do that to a guy."

"It was just a little…" Corrie strode purposefully into the dining room but came to a quick halt. Her eyes grew wide and her face went ashen. "Whoa. It looks a lot worse in the daylight."

He came to stand beside her. "Did you not see it this morning?"

"I woke up before dawn and decided to finish up the gingerbread inn before the kitchen got crowded. When your mom and Greer came in and wanted to go out to play in the snow—you know I couldn't resist that invitation. We went out the back way to keep Greer from running upstairs and waking you up."

"I am so sorry, son." His mom joined them. She took a quick look around then folded her arms and faced him with a smile. "But it's just paint, after all. It's nothing that can't be taken care of."

"Yeah, with a little time and money—two things I have very little of right now." Andy sank down to sit on the last step of the stairway and hung his head. A slow ache began to work from his tense neck muscles upward. "The painters aren't coming out today, or probably tomorrow because they don't drive in bad weather. If the snow doesn't let up, or if it affects the highways east of here, the floors won't be here on time and even if they are, if the dining room isn't ready, I can't install them. And clearly, the dining room won't be ready."

He felt as if he were literally watching his dreams crumble. Again. Last night he had told himself that he had done the right thing, making it clear to Corrie that there was no future for them. He had taken small consolation that his future rested in the completion of the Snowy Eaves Inn, and that was going to go smoothly from this point on.

Andy's shoulders slumped. He looked at Corrie then at his mother. "What happened?"

His mom came to his side and sat on the stair above his. "I came in in the middle of the night—"

Greer hung on the newel post. "I thought she was a bear—"

Corrie stood off by herself. "I only wanted to protect Greer and the inn from an intruder—"

All three of the most important females in his life spoke at once, saying nothing, really, but painting the total picture for him. He put his head in his hands. "I get it. It was an accident."

"I think it was a consequence." Greer took his hand and gave it a squeeze. "I should have believed you when you said nothing was going to get us out here and that God would watch over us."

"No, Greer, you can't take responsibility." His mother put her hand on Greer's shoulder and Andy's arm. "I showed up unannounced and barged right in."

Andy nodded. He could accept their part in this as his own failing. He should have considered the possibilities and had a contingency for them. At least Corrie hadn't…

"I actually threw the ax."

"You threw *an ax?*" He stood up. He hadn't planned on standing up but Corrie's confession drew him right out of his mellowing mood. "At my dining room?"

"At your mother, actually." She winced and bit her lower lip.

He didn't know how to respond to that. He'd welcomed her into his home, cared about her and made it very clear how much this project meant to him, how much was at stake if it got off track again. Now to hear she had done something so…thoughtless? "Are you kidding me? That's what your spur-of-the-moment, go-with-the-flow, change-plans-on-a-whim thinking led you to do? Endanger my mother? Ruin my life's work?"

"Andy, really?" His mom rose slowly, using the banister for support. "It's not ruined. It's all fixable."

"Making bad choices because you have some kooky idea that being irresponsible will keep you from *sticking* with bad choices is not fixable, Mom." He never once took his eyes off Corrie's face.

Not even when the tears began to pool in her beautiful eyes.

"I'm so sorry," she was barely able to rasp out. "I didn't mean to—"

"That's my point, Corrie." His breath eased from his constricted chest and he looked away at last. He did not raise his voice. He didn't feel angry so much as he felt defeated. He had dreamed of restoring this inn for so long, had worked toward that goal, planned, saved, hoped and when he had come to the end of his rope, prayed. And what had Corrie done? "You're not a kid. What you do should have purpose and intent. You direct your path. We all do. I don't know if I could ever... I need people in my life who understand that."

The tears rolled down her cheeks. Her lower lip quivered but she didn't say a word.

Greer moved up to take her hand but his mom intervened and guided the child away. "This is between the two of them. I think you and I should make our way home, Greer."

"There's nothing between me and Corrie, Mom. She's just in town for a contest and...her own reasons. I've got my own stuff to worry about. It's that simple." He turned away at last and looked around for his keys, his coat. He looked down and realized he didn't even have any shoes on. He headed toward the stairs to go get them. "I can pull Corrie's car out of the ditch with my truck and she can follow you back to town."

"That will take care of things once and for all then," Corrie said in a strained but controlled tone. "I'll take the gingerbread inn with me now—"

Andy stopped on the steps. "You don't have to do that."

"It's finished and I don't want it in your way," she murmured.

He did not look back. "You said the more you move it, the more chances it will crack or break or get messed up. I can bring it into town on the day you need it."

"Friday."

"Friday."

"At the community center. The entries have to be there by five but the doors open at one. The earlier you get it there the more time I have to see to any last-minute details."

"I'll be there at one," he said then went upstairs to get ready to extricate Corrie Bennington from his parking lot, his inn and his life.

Chapter Seventeen

Hannah McFarland had led the way back to Hadleyville. Once they had turned from the rural lane that made its winding way to the Snowy Eaves Inn, the going got smoother. When they left the county road to the highway, the crews had scraped and salted or plowed and pickled or whatever it was they did up here to clear away the ice and snow.

With each new phase, Corrie cried a little less. She had no business feeling so blue over Andy's rejection. He'd never pretended there could be anything more between them, never told her he trusted her or asked her to stay after the contest was over. And everything he'd said about her was certainly nothing she hadn't heard before from her mother. Maybe this time it would sink in.

"Do you have any plans for the day, Corrie?" Hannah asked when she'd seen her charge safely to the Maple Leaf Manor parking lot.

"Plans," Corrie repeated barely above a whisper. Her heart heavy, she looked at the red door of her quaint but impersonal room.

Despite everything, she did not want to be here. She wanted to be back at the inn, cleaning up, giving Andy support and encouragement and more than a few suggestions for ways to pull the place together enough to host that open house. "I think I'll snuggle down in a chair and do a little Bible study. You don't happen to know where I'd find that verse about pride going before a fall?"

"Proverbs, though that's not exactly the way it goes." Hannah smiled and put her arm around Corrie's shoulder in a sweet, motherly way. "But if you're looking for insight into my son you might do better to consider the verses about the sins of the father being visited on the sons."

"Oh?" Corrie bent down to give Greer a wave through the window then looked Andy's mom in the eye. "I don't know whether to tell you that I don't want to understand your son because after Friday I'll never see him again, or ask what you mean by that and totally blow my cover because I really do wish I *could* understand him."

She laughed and drew Corrie into a sideways hug. "Just my not too subtle way of letting you know you shouldn't be too hard on Andy. When my husband died unexpectedly, he left us in a financial bind after we had just cashed out all our savings to adopt Greer."

"So Andy grew up fast."

"He became the man of the family. He went to work for a construction company and sacrificed his college money for the good of the family. He was barely nineteen."

"That's how old my father would have been when I was born."

"Pretty young for so much responsibility. You might bear that in mind when you try to figure out what to do next."

"For Andy or my father?"

"Either one." She gave Corrie a pat on the back. "I'm just saying that sometimes it's easier to understand people if you understand their story. A thought you might want to hang on to when you talk to your mom later."

"My mom?"

"You are going to call her and tell her that you may have found your father." She wasn't asking. She was telling Corrie that she needed to do this, and she needed to do it with a forgiving, gentle heart.

"What if she's angry or hurt by that?"

"Then you'll handle it. Corrie, this is your life. You have to take charge of it. I know it sounds corny but often the truth really is so simple it's easy to dismiss it. You can't move forward with so much tying you to the past. You have to find your answers. You have to talk to your mother and find your father."

Hannah was right. She had spent the last few days dragging her feet over completing the task she'd come to Vermont to take care of because deep down she didn't want to complete it. To follow through on those goals would mean moving on, moving away from the Snowy Eaves Inn and Andy. Her father no longer lived here. She had nothing to tie her to this place now.

"Are you going to be okay?" the woman asked quietly.

"Yes." Corrie smiled for the first time since she'd left the inn and gave Andy's mom a quick hug and a thanks.

"I believe I am, because you're right, it's time for me to move on."

Corrie wasn't exactly sure what "moving on" would look like, though. She threw her coat on a chair and pulled off her boots. She looked at the phone on the nightstand, read the rate info and decided to charge her cell phone and call from that.

Stalling? Preparing, she told herself and made use of the time by looking up the verse she had angrily accused of being Andy's flaw.

She ran her finger under the words of Proverbs 16:18. "Pride goes before destruction, a haughty spirit before a fall."

She shut her eyes. She didn't know exactly how to define a haughty spirit but she was pretty sure that did not apply to the bighearted, humble man she had tried to pin it on. She exhaled slowly then started to read the passage again, only to find her gaze falling on Proverbs 16:9. "In his heart a man plans his course but the Lord determines his steps."

Corrie read the verse once, twice then another time and the tightness in her chest began to ease. *Move ahead, prepare, let the Lord direct her steps.*

The message sank into her being and filled her thoughts. She finally raised her face and said a prayer not asking for any one thing, but offering herself to God's plan and knowing it would be enough even if her mother was harsh, her father disinterested and she would never see Andy McFarland again.

"Only, if it could work out better than that, Lord, I'd think that after the birth of Jesus, of course, that was the best Christmas present of all."

Finally, Corrie was in the right frame of mind to call her mother. She took her phone and went to the window, pulling back the avocado-green curtains so that she could watch the gentle snow flurries that had moved in midday.

"Bennington's Bakery, Barbara speaking."

"You used your last name so that if he ever wanted to find you all he had to do was find a phone book, didn't you?" Corrie didn't see any reason to bother with small talk.

"I think by the time I opened the bakery he had given up looking, if he ever did. But yes, that's exactly why I used that name for the bakery. I thought even if I married again, your father could still find us," she replied. "Do you have something you want to tell me, sweetie?"

Corrie had so much she wanted to say. She wanted to tell her mother about Andy and the inn. About having the wrong name and about the mayor, and the town that she had come to love. But she had to start somewhere, so she said, "I think I found him. He lives in Virginia now."

"I see." Barbara Bennington sounded disappointed. "Is he…"

"I don't know everything, but according to Hannah McFarland, he's widowed. Never had any children."

"Never had any *other* children," her mom corrected with a flare of maternal protectiveness and a hint of melancholy. "So, you've talked to Buck then?"

"Buck? His nickname is Buck?"

"If your first name was Wallace, wouldn't you go by a nickname, too?" There was a soft laugh on the other end of the line then a hesitation. "Honey, are you trying to tell me you didn't know your father's nickname?"

"I didn't know his real name. I had it backward, James Wallace. And Buck? No clue about… Wait, you *are* the BJ loves BB that I saw carved in the beam of the attic," she had muttered.

"You found that? He wrote that there the day before I left to go back to South Carolina. We didn't know about you yet, only how we felt and what we hoped for our future together." Again, sadness tinged her mother's voice.

"But he did know about me, right, Mom?"

"He knew I was pregnant," she confirmed. "And he didn't keep his word to come for me by Christmas. My mother convinced me that he didn't deserve to know if you were a boy or girl, that unless he came to find us, he didn't care."

Corrie looked out at the snow-covered landscape and thought of that Christmas more than twenty years ago when her mother waited to hear from Wallace "Buck" James. She couldn't help comparing her feelings now for Andy and her mother's for Buck. Deep down, Corrie believed that if Andy had said he loved her, she'd have never stopped hoping that it was true. "It's because of the things Grandma said and did, not because of Buck, that you taught me that people can't trust anyone, that we only have ourselves to rely on?"

"Not trust anyone? Only count on yourself? Oh, honey, if that's what you learned from me…" Her voice trailed off in pain. "I'm so sorry. I thought by teaching you self-reliance you'd have the courage to do anything you wanted to in life, including finding Buck. I didn't want you to be like me. If I had had the courage you have shown already, by going off and looking for the things you think will give you peace of mind, make you happy, well…"

"You would have come here looking for Buck instead of waiting your whole life for him to come back to you." Corrie finished the thought. "You'd have done what made you happy, even if it meant a terrific change of plans."

When Corrie hung up she had a new understanding of her mom, and herself. The power of all the things she had learned today churned inside her head. She couldn't sit still. She looked out the window. The snow had become a fine mist only really visible in the halo of light around the Maple Leaf Manor sign.

"Snow," she whispered. "And answers. A plan and the promise that I'm not alone, that God directs my path."

She felt such peace. Andy's mother had been right. She had begun to deal with her own past and it made her feel like she could finally move ahead. Or just move *around.*

She bundled up in her coat, scarf and her beloved boots, headed out the door and hit the sidewalks of Hadleyville. All around her people were making their way around. Leaving work for the day, Christmas shopping, maybe even doing things to prepare for the contest event this weekend. Those who recognized her said hello, those she'd never met wished her Merry Christmas or warned her to keep warm.

She stayed on the main street, the same one she had traveled Friday when she had encouraged Andy to help string Christmas lights in the park. Andy's office was dark. She shivered and wrapped her scarf around her mouth and walked, her eyes fixed on the lights twinkling on the gazebo in the deepening dusk.

The wind whipped up and blew a dusting of icy snowflakes into her face. She hunched her shoulders up and looked around to see if there was a place to duck in and get warm. She realized she was on the steps of the church that Andy attended and all around her people were making their way up the steps to the big doors adorned with fresh wreaths. "The Christmas Pageant."

Her stomach lurched. She couldn't go in. She *had* to go in. Andy would be there. But then, so would Greer. Wearing the costume that Corrie had made for her.

She looked up at the door and took a deep breath.

"Hey, Corrie, come on in and sit with us, why don't you?" The mayor and her husband came up the stairs and before Corrie could protest, Great Aunt Ellie had her by the arm.

"Okay, but…if we could find a quiet spot before the pageant begins? I have something to tell you." Corrie grasped the older woman's wrist and moments later, huddled in the cramped privacy of the cloak room, Corrie shared her story and they shared a hug.

Ellie fidgeted with her glasses, obviously unsure which set she'd need to see the small numbers on the highly sophisticated phone she extracted from her coat pocket. "We have to call Buck this very minute."

"If you'd just give me his number, I can do that later. The pageant is—"

"Not going to start for almost half an hour." She settled on a pair of glasses then began moving the phone forward and back as she frowned at the screen. "I don't think I could keep this secret that long, do you, Larry?"

"Not if her life depended on it." He chuckled.

"Besides, as soon as Buck hears he won't want to waste time chatting on the phone, not when you're only going to be in town a few more days. I just know he'll want to jump in his car and come up here to talk to you in person." Ellie pressed a few numbers then extended the phone to Corrie. "Here you go."

Here she went, indeed. With each gentle purring ring in her ear Corrie imagined the sensation of a roller coaster slowly ascending the first steep climb. Crank by crank, uphill, defying gravity. Then, when it reached the peak…

"Hello, Aunt Ellie, if you're calling about Christmas, I'll be there the usual time. I won't forget. I never do," said a clear masculine voice tinged with patient good humor.

"I… This isn't your aunt. She's letting me use her phone." Corrie gulped in a quick breath and gave herself over to the roller coaster of an emotional ride. "I, uh, I don't know if you remember her but I'm Barbara Bennington's daughter."

"Of course I remember Barbie, she…I…is she all right?" Genuine concern infused his question.

That put Corrie at ease, a little. She exhaled then pushed her shoulders back. "She's… Mom is fine. Actually, I'm calling about my father."

Ellie put her arm around Corrie's shoulders for support.

"Your…father. Would I know him?"

"You are him," she said softly.

"I thought maybe you'd say that and I can't tell you how long I've waited to get this call." His voice broke.

"I know a thing or two about waiting for someone to make contact." Corrie's stomach clenched and her jaw tightened as she added, "So does my mom."

The mayor and her husband tried not to look like they were listening. She seemed suddenly fascinated by the coats hanging around them and he began examining the Christmas pageant program, but their expressions made it clear they had heard that.

"I deserve your anger and mistrust for not coming as I promised that Christmas," Buck James said in a way that shouldered the blame without excuses. "I am so sorry."

"I think that's an apology you own my mom more than me." She tried not to sound harsh but her emotions were so close to the surface. "Me, I'd just want to know why. Why didn't you come that Christmas?"

The Walkers no longer kept up the pretense of giving her privacy. Ellie folded her arms and cocked her head to show she clearly wanted to know the answer to that herself.

Corrie didn't mind, either. After all, they were family now. "Why weren't you there for my mom when I was born and for me, growing up?"

"Your grandmother didn't tell you?" He could not have faked the hurt and disbelief in the words he blurted out. Silence followed, then a deep breath. "Corrie, I don't want to turn you against your grandmother, but you should know the truth. After your mom went back to South Carolina, she contacted me and told me not to come."

Corrie felt as if she had the wind knocked out of her. "What? Why?"

"She thought I had obviously misled your mother. That none of this could have happened if I wasn't a liar and a scoundrel. She laid all the blame on me and told me that your mother and you would be better off without me." Again, his voice grew emotional and tight. "She said she'd have me arrested if I showed up at her door."

"I'm sure my mom never knew that," Corrie said softly, as much for herself as for him. Then she turned to the Walkers to say, "He tried to come. My grandmother said she'd have him arrested."

"Oh!" Ellie raised her eyebrows. "I knew it had to be something. He's a good man, Corrie."

Corrie was glad to hear that and even more glad that she truly felt it was true.

Buck cleared his throat and went on, "I was terrified, Corrie. I told myself I'd wait until things cooled down, then come. A few weeks after I thought you would have been born, I called and your grandmother told me your mother wanted no part of me and that she had made sure your mother hadn't listed me on the birth certificate so I had no legal claim on you."

"I know that's true. If your name had been there, I'd certainly have found you sooner."

"I didn't give up that easily. I tried again, but your grandmother told me that your mom had met someone else and that you didn't think of me as your father and to show up would disrupt your life irreparably."

"I believe you," she murmured, recalling her mother's story about how she had bowed to her mother's pressure. "I know Mom dated a nice man for a while but they didn't get married."

"Really?" He hesitated, and she wondered if he wanted to ask more about her mom, the woman he had loved so long ago. Instead, he said, "I did try to keep track of you, thinking one day...but then your family moved and I had no idea where. It wasn't like I could go on the internet then and track you down."

"Trust me, I've found out it isn't as easy to find a person online as they make it seem on TV." Corrie gave the mayor a smile and got one in return.

"I did try but after a while, I met someone else myself and married. We moved away because of her poor health and...and I want you to know, Corrie, I stayed away from your mom and you out of love, not out of neglect or selfishness."

"Thank you." She felt her lips move but wasn't sure she had actually gotten the words out until the mayor's husband put his hand on her shoulder to lend support.

"All I knew to do was to pray, Corrie," Buck concluded. "Pray for you and your mom, that you'd be happy and that if you wanted me in your life you'd come looking for me. Now..."

"Now I've found you," she whispered with tears streaming down her face and joy in her heart.

A few more tears, a little laughter, and a moment of gratitude to God later, Corrie handed the phone back to Ellie and hugged her again. "You were right. He'll be in town tomorrow. Thank you."

As they went into the sanctuary, Ellie practically

beamed and Corrie worried she wouldn't be able to keep their secret until Buck got to town, as they had agreed.

"Let's sit up front." Ellie lead the way to the first-row pew.

Corrie stumbled along, her boots bumping along the red carpet. The last thing she wanted was to sit front and center for the whole town to see, knowing she'd be the topic of conversation soon. Of course by whole town, she really meant one headstrong, heart-stoppingly handsome man who thought he didn't need anyone's help. She dreaded the idea of running into Andy now, feeling so vulnerable, so happy and yet so unsure. "Actually, I think I'd rather sit where I won't be noticed and can slip out if—"

She glanced back just as Andy took a seat on the last row, right by the door.

"On second thought, front row is good." She gave a meager smile and a half shrug. "If I can just slip in before anyone sees me and—"

"Corrie!" Greer appeared in the aisle at the back of the sanctuary.

Hannah McFarland waved.

Two of the men she had worked with from the park light committee raised their hands in greeting as well.

"Thanks for coming." The pageant director smiled and gave a thumbs-up. "Greer's wings look great."

"Come and see, Corrie!" Greer jumped up and did a twist at the same time trying to both talk to Corrie and at the same time show off the wings that Corrie had designed, but been unable to finish.

Corrie started to say something about having to get her seat with the mayor before the pew filled up.

"Go," Ellie urged. "We'll save you a seat."

Greer and Hannah both motioned to a sliver of space next to Andy, clearly offering for Corrie to join him on Andy's behalf.

She couldn't join him, of course. She suspected he knew that. She had come so far and finally figured out what she had been looking for for so long. She wanted a home. She wanted a place where she was accepted for herself. She wanted to be of help to others.

She wouldn't find those with Andy and sitting next to him in his church would only make her feel that more keenly. Still, she owed it to Greer to go and tell her how good she looked and to Andy to tell him she'd see him Friday.

"If y'all will excuse me for a second, I'll be right back," she told the mayor.

"Did you hear that, Larry? Y'all. I think I've heard Buck say y'all since he moved to Virginia. Isn't it nice to know that when they meet there won't be a language barrier?" She laughed.

Corrie put her finger to her lips to remind the mayor they weren't talking about the news yet then she went and spent a few seconds admiring Greer's wings and accepting Hannah's appreciation for having done most of the work on the costume. When the pair of them hurried off to get Greer in position for her role in the production, Corrie turned to Andy.

"I think I owe you an apology." He leaned against the pew in front of him with both hands and hung his head then met her gaze. "I was pretty tough on you this morning."

"Not surprising, considering how tough you are on yourself. " She wished she could reach out and give his arm a squeeze but she restrained the impulse. "I messed up, Andy. I acted rashly."

"You were trying to protect my sister. I was out of line."

Corrie decided not to argue that point. "How bad is the damage to the inn?"

He shook his head. "Gonna set me back a couple more days on top of the couple I've already lost and at least a grand to pay for extra workers. And because even if the floors could get here through the snow, we won't have time to install them, more money to do some temporary flooring."

She felt just awful about that. "If I had it, I'd write you a check right now."

He cocked his head, studying her. "I know you would but I couldn't accept it."

She cast her eyes down to the toes of her boots. "I know you wouldn't."

They stood there as people shuffled around them, friends chatting with each other, shaking hands, families laughing and settling into the pews.

Not having anything more to add, or rather knowing there was nothing more he would accept from her, she looked back toward the mayor. "Well…"

He gave a jerk of his head to acknowledge Larry and Ellie. "Did you get a chance to call your father yet?"

"Just now." She couldn't help breaking into a broad grin.

"Really?"

"He's coming here tomorrow but we're not going to tell anyone until we've had a chance to talk. He's going to bring photos to show me about that time and his life." Suddenly feeling warm, she worked the buttons of her coat free and flapped the lapels to get some air. Only it wasn't the church that had her flushed, it was Andy's steady, unreadable gaze. "I only wish…"

"That you still had the snow globe?" He finished for her.

"I was going to say that I had photos of my life to share. The snow globe, that was between him and Mom. I'm not sure it would be *my* place to have brought it to him." A family of six came bustling by, nudging Corrie forward, almost into Andy's side. She pulled back, trying to sound perfectly unruffled by his closeness as she concluded, "By the way, we had a good talk, my mom and me. She told me a little about that time, about the role my grandmother played in keeping her from following her heart and how that made her push me to be so independent. I think she feels some guilt about it."

"I hope your mom is able to work through that. Unfinished business can have some far-reaching effects," he said, his jaw tense.

"I kind of got the feeling, talking to both of them that there *is* unfinished business between them and that they both have regrets." Corrie knew the man spoke from experience. "I'm not sure what *I* can do about that. "

"Maybe I could…" He started to reach out to her but another stream of people pressed by and the minister took the pulpit to ask everyone to take a seat so the pageant could begin.

"I promised I'd sit with the mayor and her husband." Corrie pointed in their direction.

"Don't let me keep you."

Keep me, she wanted to say. Her heart sank when he gave her a smile and a nod then stepped away and sat back down.

She gave him a small wave then took her seat. The pageant went off pretty much as it had in rehearsal. The kids were adorable. The music joyful. The company was warm. Except for the heavy pain in her chest every time she thought about Andy, it was one of the sweetest Christmas moments she'd ever had.

When the last strains of music faded, the children filed out with their small flashlights held like lit candles. Corrie's gaze followed Greer all the way to the doorway. When the lights in the sanctuary came up, Corrie naturally sought Andy's seat. It was empty. He must have rushed off, probably wanting to get back to work.

He had sat through the pageant alone and left alone. Just the way he planned to restore the inn, or lose everything if the inn couldn't be done in time.

It didn't have to be that way. She looked around at all the wonderful people who had embraced her and who were so clearly proud of their community and part of a spiritual fellowship that loved and supported each other. This is what it felt like to have a home, Corrie knew now.

She had her answers. She wanted a way to help Andy find his.

Chapter Eighteen

He was right.

Andy *knew* he was right.

You had to prepare in life. You couldn't just make stuff up as you went along. You had to look at the big picture, cover all the angles and be ready for everything, even what you didn't see coming. You couldn't take your eyes off the goal.

That's what he'd done. Taken his eyes off the goal, gotten tangled up trying to go too many directions at once. That's how he got in this fix. He'd gotten distracted and now his life's work was a shambles. For all this striving to do otherwise, he hadn't done any better than his father taking care of his family.

He opened the passenger door of his truck and looked down at the gingerbread replica of the Snowy Eaves Inn. The perfect vision of all Corrie wanted it to be, and *he* had hoped it could be.

And never would be.

He shook his head. Even if the painters hadn't bugged out on him, if the flooring company had been able to meet the deadline, he and Corrie wouldn't have come to any different conclusion. She had to go back to South Carolina. Staying here did not fit in either of their plans.

Andy was right.

Nothing could change that.

Andy wasn't in the business of change, after all. He fixed things. If he could, he restored them but that didn't change the past. Still, it often went a long way toward healing it.

He paused and looked around the parking lot. Corrie's small car was already here, parked right beside a slightly bigger car with Virginia tags. He raised his head and searched his surroundings. He was looking for something in particular, *someone* in particular, but couldn't help noticing that for all the cars in the lot today, there weren't any people to be seen.

He didn't get a chance to give it much thought though, as the car he'd been looking for came rolling into the lot. He gave a wave. The car pulled up next to him. After a few quick introductions, thank yous, reassurances and some hastily laid plans, he got a good grip on the snowy landscaped base of the gingerbread inn and slid it from his truck.

A woman with a nametag designating her as a volunteer flung open the outer door of the community center when he got to it. She directed him to a swinging door with a big banner over it proclaiming: Hadleyville Holiday Gingerbread House Showcase.

1 p.m., just as promised. Andy turned around to back through with his delivery. Once he'd made it, then he'd go back to his truck and bring Corrie what he'd spent the

last two days working on as a goodbye present. Goodbye dreams. Goodbye inn. Goodbye—

"Christmas at the Snowy Eaves Inn!" Corrie Bennington rushed to the door and held it open for him as she made a quick circle with her finger to coax him to turn around.

He didn't want to take his eyes off her. Nothing could have prepared him for the power of just seeing here there, smiling that bright smile that reached all the way to the beautiful eyes behind those red frames. He had expected he'd show up, drop off the entry and leave his parting gift for her. They'd be settled up and free to go their separate ways.

She made the motion again then extended her arm and whispered, "Follow my lead, okay?"

He hesitated for only a moment then gave in, because as slapdash as it had been, that was the plan. That was what he'd said he'd do. He turned slowly and stepped over the threshold into the brightly lit room.

"It's here, y'all!" Corrie called out from behind him.

She extended her arm as though she was presenting her entry for all the world to see.

And from the cheer that rose up and all the familiar faces greeting him, she was presenting it to just about everyone in his world.

"What's going on?" he asked, as he scanned the grinning faces of the mayor, the sheriff, the members of his church, his mom and sister and Buck James. "Is every entry in the contest getting this treatment?"

"Nope, because this isn't a contest entry anymore."

She moved around in front of him and walked backwards motioning for him to keep moving as she directed.

He couldn't make sense of what she had said or what she was doing but he didn't really care. It was Corrie, smiling instead of fragile and unhappy as he'd last seen her and wearing those dopey boots. So he smiled back at her and asked, "What do you mean this isn't a contest entry? Did you withdraw?"

"I had to or be disqualified. You see in those rules you so rightly pointed out I had to follow, it clearly states that relatives of anyone on the panel of judges are not eligible to enter. And since the head judge is my great aunt Ellie…"

The mayor tipped her head in acknowledgment.

"Oh, um, Andy McFarland, this is my father," she extended her hand toward a man that Andy had met years ago at the annual Christmas Eve Open House and the Snowy Eaves Inn. "Buck James."

"I'd shake your hand but…" He lifted the gingerbread inn slightly.

"Oh!" Corrie moved to a table at the front of the room and patted it to let him know where to set the gingerbread replica of the inn that he would probably have to put up for sale after the first of the year. She squared her shoulders and adjusted her red glasses. "I can't enter the contest. But that puts me in the perfect spot to do this."

She spun around and raised her hands. "If y'all will kindly gather 'round. I'd like to offer to my version of the local landmark, the Snowy Eaves Inn, for sale to the highest bidder."

"There's something more…bidder?" He came up

behind her and muttered in her ear. "What are you doing?"

She glanced back over her shoulder. "I'm proving to you that you can trust me, Andy. I made that mess in your inn and cost you time and money. I plan to raise the money for the extra man-hours to clean it up and put it right, even if I have to provide some of those man-hours with my own two womanly little hands."

"That's a kind gesture, Corrie." Kinder than he deserved after the way he'd treated her. "But I don't think anyone would pay enough money for a gingerbread house to even begin—"

"I bid one hundred dollars," called out one of the grizzled old bench setters that Corrie had charmed at the park-decorating project.

"Why would you pay that much for a house you can't sleep in or eat?" one of his compatriots demanded.

"I like pretty things," he said without cracking a smile. "Besides, I went to my high school prom up there. Holds a sentimental value for me."

"Well, I was married there and my wife tells me it holds *more* sentimental value for *me*—or else. So I bid two hundred."

The numbers ran up fast. Three hundred. Four hundred. Five.

Andy couldn't believe it. They already had enough to bring in a couple more guys to get the painting and trim work done. If he and his mom and Corrie pitched in, they'd have it done in no time.

"I do appreciate this but the floors aren't going to get here in time because of the snow," he told her even as he watched Jim Walker break up a dispute between two determined bidders over who deserved to have the honor of casting the highest bid right down to the penny and ending the proceedings without further ado. "Then there's the issue of tablecloths and drapes. We can't pull the place together for Christmas Eve."

"We can, if we work together. I came up with some solutions if you're open to hearing them."

She was asking him if was capable of accepting a change of plans. He anchored his work boots on the brightly polished floor, folded his arms and narrowed his eyes at her. "I'm listening."

"We paint the concrete with the wrong color gray paint and sprinkle glitter over it. It will be lovely lit by the tree, the fireplace and candles on the tables." Her eyes shone just describing it. "And we use those spare gold-colored bedspreads and curtains and we can use the sheets for tablecloths, maybe with some gold sheer fabric as runners. What do you think?"

"I think you're right." He looked deep into her eyes. "You can make it all come together, Corrie."

"Sold for one thousand two-hundred, fifty-seven dollars and eighteen cents to…everyone who made a donation." Larry Walker raised a basket full of cash and pledges and the whole crowd erupted in a cheer.

The whole town had just pitched in to help him get the inn ready in time. "Why would they do this?"

"Because you aren't the only one who cares about that inn, Andy. You showed me that when you took me to the town museum and when we went into the attic and saw all the names of people who wanted to leave a little bit of themselves behind there. People here love that place and they'd like to help you, if you'd let them." She took his hand, stole a look at the crowd that had now moved their focus from the fight for the inn to the fight Corrie was putting up, trying to get through to him. "It's all right, you know, to ask for help."

"I know," he said. He felt both humbled and heroic all at once because he knew something Corrie couldn't possibly know. He turned, brushed her hair off the corner of her glasses and then touched her cheek. "I already did ask for help—twice."

"When?"

He couldn't take his eyes from her face. Up until this moment he had thought of himself as in charge. He thought he had come up with the game plan and carried it out according to his own directions. But here now, standing amidst these people he cared for, looking into the eyes of the woman he loved, he knew the truth. "I asked for help on the night you blew into my life."

"Really? How did you do that?"

"In a prayer." He tensed slightly and shut his eyes to add, "And, Greer, that does not mean this is the answer to your prayer that I get a girlfriend, because—"

"She's not your girlfriend," the group supplied in a weary but disbelieving singsong.

"I was going to say, because that's not the real answer," he said loud and clear. "The real answer is that God heard what was in my heart and by laying my deepest desires at His feet, He moved through me. He prepared me for an unexpected answer."

"Does that mean you've had a change of heart?" she murmured through a soft smile, her eyes shining with unshed tears.

"That means I am open to a change of plans," he

whispered back. "Corrie, I was so wrong. Wrong about you. Wrong about not letting people help me, even if that meant they sometimes let me down. And I was wrong to ever let you walk out of the inn without telling you that no matter how much I did to restore the place, it would always feel incomplete without you in it."

"Oh, Andy." She threw her arms around his neck.

"And because I promised you the night we met that I'd put things right about your snow globe, I asked for help again yesterday." He got out his phone and sent a quick text.

Corrie tried to steal a peek but he whisked his phone out of sight then turned to the crowd.

"As for the part about Corrie being my girlfriend…" He shifted Corrie so that he could look her in the eyes as he said, "As for Corrie being my girlfriend? She'd have to be open to staying in Vermont and helping me not just get the inn ready for Christmas Eve, but for every day after."

She beamed up at him. "I could do that."

"Kiss her!" someone in the group called out.

"Not until she tells me her plans."

"I plan to follow my heart and let God order my steps. I plan to trust you, Andy McFarland but I can't stay in Vermont unless you can promise me the same things."

"I promise," he said softly just before he kissed her.

The crowd sighed, cheered, applauded again.

Andy felt self-conscious and pulled away, whispering in her ear, "I love you, Corrie Bennington. I know it's only been a week, but I've never been so sure of anything in my life."

"I love you, too," she whispered. "And I love this town. It feels like home but I'm not sure how my mom will feel about me moving here."

"Then ask her." He took Corrie by the shoulders and turned her around to face a round-faced woman with strawberry-blond hair holding a small box before her and walking as though trying to maneuver on a tight rope.

"Barbie?" Buck James stepped out of the crowd.

"Hello, Buck," the woman said with a shy smile and flushed cheeks. "I guess we have a lot of catching up to do."

"Oh, Andy." Tears rolled down Corrie's face.

Andy took the box from Barbara's hands. "I worked on this all day and night to make it all better for you, Corrie."

Corrie lifted the lid off the box, reached down inside.

"I couldn't make it a snow globe again, so I…"

"You improvised," she whispered then looked up from the rescued Snowy Eaves Inn that had been in the snow globe all these years, now in a glass and wood case.

"It still plays music and if you press this button…" He reached beneath the box, wound the music box and pushed a button that started a tiny fan. Glitter began to swirl and fly all around the box like a blizzard of sparkling fresh snow.

"I love it. You didn't just fix it, you made it better," she told him, then she looked from her gift to her parents then up at Andy again.

"I could say the same about you." He kissed her

lightly again and pulled her close in a tight embrace so he could whisper in her ear, "You have made everything better, Corrie. I love you and I hope we spend Christmas Eve at the Snowy Eaves Inn for many, many, many Christmases to come."

Epilogue

◠❧

Christmas Eve, one year later.

"I like this tree better than last year's." Greer circled the nearly ten-foot-tall elegant fir tree, lit with hundreds of colored lights, dozens of ornaments sent from guests who had visited from all over the country, and yards of fat, shimmering garland.

"Not me." Andy looped his arms around Corrie and pulled her back against him. "What do you think, *Mrs. McFarland?*"

"Mmmm." She shut her eyes and reveled in the joy of celebrating this special night in her husband's embrace. "I think I can't get enough of hearing my new name."

"Aww, you've had it for three whole months. Enough with the lovey-dovey stuff already." Greer crinkled up her nose and tilted her head back to examine the tree again. "This tree does need something, though."

"Any news on when our special guests will arrive?" Hannah came into the lobby, passed the tree and gazed out in the direction of the drive. She wouldn't be able to see anything even in the late afternoon light because of the trees and the light snow.

"The open house starts at seven and will be done in time for us to go to our eleven o'clock candlelight church service, same as always." Andy moved to Corrie's side, keeping his strong arm around her shoulders.

"I didn't mean open house guests." Hannah shot him a motherly backward glance. "I mean Corrie's parents."

"Parents," Corrie murmured. "There's another word I can't hear often enough."

Hannah rounded the tree in the opposite direction of her daughter, giving the tree a once-over as she did. "I bet we'll have another wedding this coming year, what do you think?"

Corrie could hardly contain her giddiness at the possibility. She had met her father for the first time a year ago. Her mother and Buck met again after all these years in the place they had fallen in love. There was so much to deal with, so much heartache and so many mistakes.

Corrie had always known that her mother carried hard feelings toward Buck. But also learned that she had always struggled with the conflict of having a child she loved with all her heart and that she had had that child out of wedlock. That went a long way toward her understanding her mother even more. Once their relationship had begun to grow, her mom came to Vermont to visit more. So did Buck.

After Corrie and Andy's wedding three months ago, her parents began dating.

Corrie inhaled deeply the scent of pine and wonderful foods and her husband's fresh aftershave clinging to his wool sweater. She looked around at the stairway and the concrete floors that had turned out so well they decided to save a bunch of money and not cover them with wood. She had come down that staircase to marry the man she loved, right here, in front of these windows where the tree now stood.

"I think you're right," Hannah said as she joined her young daughter looking up at the towering tree before them. "It does need something."

"A star?" Andy asked, pointing to the bare tippy-top branch.

"How about a Sarah Finn?" Corrie teased, giving her new sister-in-law a wink.

"I know its seraphim, now." she said, sounding quite grown up. "And that gives me an idea."

She ran off toward the room where she and her mother were spending the night so that the whole family could be together on Christmas morning.

"Family," Corrie whispered.

"Hmm?" Andy crooked his finger under her chin.

"I was just thinking about why this tree *might* actually be better than last year's—because it's the first one I'll ever share with my whole family."

"But not the only one you'll share with your adoring husband." He gave her a kiss.

She smiled to think of the small tree with the home-made trimming they had in their room upstairs. "Much as I love the idea of the whole family, there is something to be said for—"

"The perfect tree topper." Greer came sliding across the floor holding up the old sock monkey Andy had given her and she had clung to for the last few years. "Buddy Mon-Kay!"

She had dressed him again in the angel's robe, halo and wings she'd fashioned for him last year.

"A sock monkey?" Andy asked, still keeping his arm around Corrie.

"Not just any sock monkey. It's a family heirloom, like the Snowy Eaves Inn snow globe," she told him, holding the toy up high. "We're supposed to pass it along. You gave it to me when you didn't need it. And now that Mom is staying in the country to work, I don't need it to keep me company anymore, so I am passing it along."

"That's a lovely idea, sweetie," Corrie bent down to look the child in the face, and realized she didn't have to bend nearly as much as she had a year ago. "But who are you passing it along to?"

"Your kid!" She went up on tiptoe and and motioned toward the top branch indicating the monkey should be installed immediately.

Corrie stood bolt upright.

"We don't have a kid," Andy hurried to say.

"And we don't have any plans for one," Corrie hastened to add.

"I know. That's why it's going up on the tree this year. By next year, though, who knows?"

Andy gave her a squeeze and chuckled. "Who knows?"

She turned and looked into her husband's eyes. She no longer blushed when she stood so close to him but her heart fluttered. "In his heart a man plans his course but the Lord determines his steps."

"I love you, Corrie Bennington McFarland," he whispered. "Merry Christmas."

"Merry Christmas, Andy," she murmured in response. Then she kissed her new husband, helped him put the monkey up as a tree topper then welcomed her parents to their home to celebrate the greatest gift of all, God's love.

* * * * *

Dear Reader,

The idea for this book first came from watching Gingerbread House contests and from admiring the houses in The Red Scooter, an antique mall owned by a friend in Taylorsville, Ky. But later it also became about finding someone and about how loss and hope shape who we become.

That became timely when I found one of my dearest friends from high school online this past year. At first it was just fun to catch up. Then we began to talk about our children and she shared with me how her faith had guided and comforted her life. Then in November, her sole surviving son died unexpectedly from an undetected heart ailment and it seemed such a small token on my part but also a blessing to be able to remember him in this letter and dedication.

Theo was born on June 14, 1991 (Flag Day—he thought the flags were out for him) and died November 11, 2009. I didn't know Theo except through his writing and his mom. Reading his poetry and lyrics, I know he was a gentle, sweet soul with so much promise, gone too soon. I know he was loved by his parents every moment of his life and every moment that their hearts beat, he will be there with his other siblings, who went before him to the Lord.

So as you read this letter and this book, I hope you say a prayer for those who are no longer with us, those who will always love us and when you see the flags out on Flag Day, you smile knowing that Theo Anderson will be celebrating in heaven.

Annie Jones

QUESTIONS FOR DISCUSSION

1. The hero, heroine and his sister all consider the issue of how God answers prayer in this story. How do you think God answers prayer?

2. As a grown child, the heroine sees her upbringing in a different light than her mother thought she was raising her. Why do you think it happens between parents and children?

3. The heroine's mother tried to shape her child by forcing her to be independent but the heroine reacted by being more open to the help of others. Does this reflect parent/child relationships you know?

4. Do you see ways in which the heroine actually is making life choices that are in keeping with her mother's goal of being independent?

5. The main characters struggle with their approach to getting things done—planning versus flying by the seat of your pants. Which are you? Do you think that is an obstacle to a relationship?

6. The hero and heroine also have differing views about small churches being involved in their lives, she is grateful for it but he finds himself hiding in a back pew to avoid matchmakers. What do you think is the best amount of involvement between church members?

7. The heroine has a snow globe of the Snowy Eaves Inn. Do you have a memento of a place you've never been but dream of one day seeing?

8. Have you ever used homemade Christmas decorations on your tree? What were they?

9. The heroine comes a long way to look for her father but then does things to keep from being able to follow through. Why do you think she does this?

10. Have you ever tried to make a gingerbread house? Tell about how it turned out.

11. The hero reacted to his father's sudden death by trying to control situations to protect his family. What were the flaws in this plan?

12. How did you find the characters' faith affecting their choices and relationships?

13. How do you think you apply the verse Proverbs 16:9 (In his heart a man plans his course but the Lord determines his steps.) in your life?

14. How do you think the characters demonstrated this verse?

15. In the end, the heroine proved to the hero that he could trust her by making a sacrifice to help pay for the mess she'd made. How does this demonstrate not just her love for him but also how her faith becomes a part of that love?